DAVID HANKINS

Lost Bard Enterprises

Death and the Taxman

by David Hankins

EBook ISBN: 978-1-962740-02-9
Trade Paperback ISBN: 978-1-962740-00-5
Dust Jacket Hardcover ISBN: 978-1-962740-01-2
Cover design by Sarah Morrison

Second Printing – December 2024

Published by
Lost Bard Enterprises LLC
PO Box 32
Bettendorf, IA 52722
david@davidhankins.com

To Beatrix, my first and most enthusiastic fan.

To Michelle, my rock. Thank you for believing in me.

To any tax auditors reading this: you are lovely people.
Please don't audit me again.

Also by David Hankins

Grimsworld

Death and the Taxman
Death and the Dragon
Death and the Immortal
(Coming 2026)

Grimsworld Tales
(Companion Collection)

These books and more available at
www.davidhankins.com

CONTENTS

Chapter 1

A CUP OF TEA

I, THE GRIM REAPER, terror of men's souls, shall forever-more despise Mondays because that was the day I met Frank Totmann. That was the day I *became* Frank Totmann.

I found him having a heart attack in his dingy office on the third floor of the 'Colorado Springs Internal Revenue Service Tax Assistance Center.' What a mouthful. They should have named it 'The Land of Evil Auditors.'

Frank's office was a testament to his career in government service. Achievement awards displayed in cheap frames. A battered wooden desk covered in tax audits, sticky notes, and knick-knacks. No family photos. Just a picture of a fluffy white cat with a scrunched face. Frank himself was a balding pudgy man without a single sharp edge. His brown tweed suit strained its buttons, its leather elbow patches worn and scuffed. A short salt-and-pepper beard hid his jowls, but not his pained grimace.

I twisted my scythe *Grace* and stopped time. Frank gasped. He clutched his chest and drew relieved breaths. I pointed a bony finger, let my eye sockets flame a bit for effect, and intoned, "Frank Totmann, your time has come."

Frank sat back, drew more calming breaths, then threw me a broad smile. "Cup of tea before we go?" He produced a thermos and two teacups from under the desk.

How touching. Nobody ever offered refreshments. It's a lonely half-life, being Death, so I enjoy sharing folks' final moments. They usually complain about being too young to die or attempt to cheat me, but I don't mind. They're the only conversations I have. I nodded with gravity and grace.

What a fool I was. Never accept tea from a dying auditor.

I turned corporeal, took a sip, and coughed. It tasted of

blood and ashes. Abrupt pain seared my bones, dropping me to my knees. The world spun, went dark, and with a distressing stretch which ended in a *pop,* I found myself sitting in Frank's chair staring across the desk at ... me.

I blinked, shocked to have eyelids, and blinked again. No, that wasn't me. Frank Totmann's spirit, a mirror image of the body I now possessed, grinned stupidly in Death's cowl. In *my* cowl, clutching *my* scythe—crafted by the Devil and blessed by the Almighty. It gave me the power to parse human souls.

Of all the *cheek.*

I lunged across the desk, caught my hip on its edge, and sprawled across audit reports and tax returns. Breath whooshed out of me. Unfamiliar with a human body, I forgot to breathe in. Stars flashed before my eyes.

Frank jumped back, holding my scythe high like a bully taunting a child. *Grace's* ebony handle twisted in his grip and time resumed. I flopped onto his chair, which rolled back with plastic protests, and sucked in a breath. My heart pounded in my chest. Frank's chest. Whatever.

I grabbed the spilled teacup and sniffed it. It smelled of anise, copper, and ... *magic.* My eyes went wide. "How?" I asked, then flinched. The Grim Reaper should boom and intone, not squeak like a scared bureaucrat.

Frank's grin became a smirk. "Ancient soul transfer spell. Sumerian, I think. Doc said my heart was failing, so I nailed the timing of your arrival by taking poison. We shared the transference potion and voila"—he took a bow—"I cheated Death."

I flung the teacup at the wall. It shattered and fell to the industrial carpet. How the hell had an IRS auditor unearthed a Sumerian soul transfer spell?

How dare he use it on *me*? On *Death*?

And after offering hospitality. Never again! Never again would I...

My mouth opened and closed like a dying fish as the gravity of the situation hit home.

Never again was right. I was a human. A flesh and blood human. Mortal.

More importantly, I was a mortal who—I checked my internal clock which measured human lives—should have died five minutes ago. My gaze flicked to Frank. To the scythe in his hands.

He followed my gaze to *Grace* and shook his head. "I'm not reaping your soul. Not even sure how, to tell the truth. But"—he twirled my scythe then swung it like a golf club—"I'll get the hang of it. Besides, that body's not dead. I spiked my tea with the poison's antidote." He waggled his fingers at me, said, "See ya!" and drifted through the door.

I slouched in the chair, dumbfounded for the first time in millennia. The Rules were quite clear. Frank's soul was supposed to cross over today. I had to swap us back, restore the balance before Hell's bureaucrats noticed. Before the Auditor—Hell's Auditor—noticed and took *my* soul instead.

***

I sat in Frank's office for an hour, my mind chasing its tail. How do I, the Grim Reaper, cheat death? This heart may have resumed beating, but it couldn't last long. My hands, used to clutching my scythe, grasped at the air. I grabbed a pen and clicked it obsessively.

It wasn't the same.

The Auditor worried me. Hell's final arbiter of the Rules, those stringent strictures that governed all spiritual matters, was not known for leniency. He was the model upon which the profession of auditors was built. If he discovered me stripped of my power, bereft of the protection of Death's identity, he would drag me into Hell's darkest pit and throw away the key.

We have ... history.

The Rules forbade spirits from interfering with Death's duties or, by extension, with Death himself. But I was no longer Death. Merely a displaced soul in the soon-to-be corpse of a tax auditor. My cowl and my scythe were gone, and I had no clue how to get them back.

What chaos would Frank Totmann wreak in my stead? Would he reap the wrong souls? Open the gates of Abaddon? Bring the Nephilim and Demigods back to Earth? Would he *fail* to reap souls? Heavens, even the mere possibility...

A knock at the door interrupted my spiraling thoughts. A short, solid woman with pinned-back graying hair swung the door open. She wore a matronly flowered dress, an overabundance of clattering jewelry, and a smile that lit her face like she was genuinely pleased to see me.

That was a new experience.

"Staying late, Frank?" Her voice was warm, like honey. Her lotus flower perfume overwhelmed the lingering scent of anise in the air.

I clicked the pen a few more times and read her soul through dark brown eyes. Cordelia Knowles, fifty-eight years old, death in forty-three years. "Uh, no," I said and rose awkwardly.

"Walk me to my car?"

"Sure, uh, Cordelia."

Her brows knit together. "It's Cora. I told you on our first date." Her voice slowed and she tilted her head. "You okay, Frank? You look like death warmed over."

You have no idea. Aloud I tried to say, 'I'm fine,' but the words stuck in my throat. I grimaced. Bloody Archangel Gabriel and his bloody restrictions. He'd burned the words 'Honesty in Death' into my soul when he made me the Reaper.

I couldn't lie.

An agent of both Heaven and Hell must remain above reproach. I'd never chafed under that restriction before today.

After flapping my jowls again like that bloody dying fish, I said, "I'm alive. That's what's important." I stomped around the desk and followed Cora into the hall. She gave me a piercing look but didn't press as we entered a cubicle farm with people streaming toward an elevator.

The room was a large square, broad and deep but with a low drop-ceiling. Scuffed industrial carpet matched Frank's office. A mixture of perfume, sweat, and mildew filled the air. Ah, the smell of the bottom rung of government service.

Chest-high gray cubicle walls under harsh fluorescent lights made the room look like a human-sized rat's maze. Cheerful banter near the elevator said the rats were excited for their escape, but they'd return to the maze tomorrow. And the day after. And the day after that. The vicious cycle would only end when I paid them their final visit.

Cora chattered about work as we followed the crowd, and my thoughts turned inward.

Frank had found a Sumerian spell to swap our souls. There had to be a reversal. But where would he keep it? Here?

I glanced around. Not likely.

His home then. I nodded to myself. Yes, that was the ticket. Find Frank's house, retrieve his spell book, and get out of this body.

Cora guided me around the crowd to a door beside the elevator marked EXIT. I reached it first and tried to pass through.

Like I always do.

My face smacked into solid wood, and I bounced off, popping the door open. I stumbled back, hands flying to my nose. "Ow!"

The crowd by the elevator burst into laughter with a smattering of applause. Someone called, "Been walking long, Frank?"

"No," I said, rubbing my nose and glaring at the offending door as it swung back toward me. The laws of physics were so ... inconvenient. Cora placed a comforting hand on my shoulder, and we pushed into the stairwell. Plain white walls and cement steps greeted us.

"Frank? Are you sure you're okay?" Cora asked.

I patted her hand noncommittally and headed downstairs. At the bottom, I was careful to press on the push bar before stepping outside. I felt inordinately pleased with myself when it worked.

Bright sunlight made me blink. The city of Colorado Springs rose on foothills, climbing partway up an imposing ridgeline. The cool wind that plucked at my suit was crisp and filled with the light scent of autumn. I drew a deep, invigorating breath. I drew another, feeling alive in a way I'd never known. Cora hooked my elbow and guided me toward her rusty Peugeot. I recognized the car because I'd reaped a soul from one last week. In midair. It had blown through an Alpine guardrail to plummet off a cliff. The deceased had blamed the car for his demise, never mind the half-written text on his cell phone.

"Well, this is me," Cora said, fishing keys from her purse. "Are we on for tonight?"

"To ... night?"

"Yes, silly. Dinner? At Edelweiss? You never confirmed our plans, but I thought, you know, since you said you'd never tried schnitzel..."

"I have not tried schnitzel." I spoke with finality, reveling in an easy truth.

She gave me a bemused smile and said, "Well then, that's settled." She opened her door, then paused as if waiting. Her brown eyes locked with mine and then, to my horror, she rocked forward and pecked me on the lips. Blood rushed to Cora's cheeks, and she slid into her car. "See you at seven!" She waved and was gone. I stood there, dumbfounded for the second time.

She'd kissed me. I ... I'd never been kissed. It felt odd, this mashing of body parts together, and left my lips feeling tingly. Perhaps it was the wind. Yes, that was it.

I gave myself a shake. No time for that now. Find Frank's house; reverse the spell. Stay focused on what mattered before the Auditor found out and banished me to the Realm of Torments. Forever.

Chapter 2

SIX MINUTES OF TERROR

I'D REAPED TOO MANY souls from crumpled wrecks to try driving myself. Best leave that to the experts. I headed for the nearest road to find a cab. Traffic flowed past in a noisy blur. Cars, trucks, busses. Six lanes of chaos that reeked of exhaust and precipitous urgency. I raised a hand, but nobody stopped. A chrome-laden motorcycle rumbled past, and its heavily bearded rider waved at me.

Not helpful.

But my hand was up anyway. I waved back.

A cabbie finally saw me. A yellow sedan whipped across two lanes and rocked to a stop, tires scraping the curb. I carefully opened the car door as Cora had done.

Success. I was getting the hang of this human thing.

"Where to, pal?" the cabbie asked. He had short sandy-colored hair and a lopsided smile that matched the identification card on the seatback. I automatically checked his soul through his cheerful gray eyes. Louis Faretti, thirty-six, death in seven years.

"The home of Frank Totmann, Louis," I said, sliding inside. The cab smelled of industrial cleaners and artificial lemon with a whiff of vomit. The bench seats were cracked leather, and the carpeted floorboards were mottled with so many stains that I couldn't identify their original color.

Louis hung one arm over the bench seat. "Got an address, bud?"

I blinked at him then rummaged through Frank's pockets. Wallet, keys, cell phone. I dug into the wallet, found something with Frank's picture and address, and read it aloud. Louis nodded and sped away, tires screeching. Horns blared as we wove violently through traffic.

Over the next six minutes of terror, I discovered why the cab smelled of vomit. I managed, barely, to keep my gorge down as Louis chatted.

"Whatcha do for a living?"

"For the living, nothing. The dead are my concern." I clutched the door as we zoomed around a truck.

"Coroner? Huh. Never drove a coroner before." He glanced in his rearview. A cardboard apple tree under the mirror danced to the erratic tune of his driving. "You're looking kinda pale, bud. Rough day at the office? Someone send you a body that wasn't quite dead yet?" He chuckled and slammed on the brakes as traffic stopped around us. I rocked forward and caught myself on his seat.

"Uh, yes," I said, falling back as the cab shot forward and resumed weaving through traffic. "He stole something very valuable." My scythe, my cowl, my very identity as Death. "Failure to retrieve it will have dire consequences." Eternal torments. I shuddered.

Louis's eyes went wide. "A real Lazarus story, but with a twist. Ain't that wild? So, what, you gonna get fired?" I glowered at the back of Louis's head. Lazarus was a fluke. Divine intervention which ruined my perfect record and nearly led to an audit. The motorcyclist I'd seen earlier honked and made a rude gesture as Louis cut him off. We passed into the ridgeline's shadow and the temperature dropped.

"Worse," I said. "I could face Judgment." Judgment long delayed for my original sin. My mind shied away from that train of thought.

We screeched to a stop before a sad-looking house with cracked tan siding and brown grass. Loose gutters overflowed with leaves and peeling blue paint on the door revealed patches of red underneath. There was no garden, just a pair of low bushes bracketing the house's corners and a single spindly cottonwood tree in the middle of the yard. Everything had a common theme of 'unhealthy and dying.' Horticulture and home maintenance clearly weren't Frank's strong suits.

"That'll be twelve bucks even," Louis said.

I blinked at him then remembered. Money. Humans used money for everything. I handed him Frank's wallet.

Louis arched an eyebrow and retrieved some bills before handing it back. He passed me a card. "If you need a ride, give me a ring." His head cocked to one side. "Never caught your name, friend."

"Grim Reaper." I fumbled at the door handle, which was different from the one outside the car.

Louis barked a laugh. "Man, your parents had a twisted

sense of humor. No wonder you became a coroner."

The door finally popped open, and I tumbled out.

"See ya, Grim!" Louis waved, and I slammed the door. As he sped off, I set my jaw and approached Frank's house.

Getting inside proved challenging. Why was *every* door handle different? This one had a stupid little knob that wouldn't turn.

Keys, right.

The door creaked open, releasing an overwhelming stench of old coffee and stale sweat. I stepped inside, and my eyes adjusted to the dim interior.

Frank's cramped living room looked much like his office: cheap and cluttered. Clothes, dishes, and detritus littered every surface. A massive television dominated the righthand wall, looming over a stained brown couch and a coffee table piled high with pizza boxes, aluminum cans, and Heaven-knows what else.

I wrinkled my nose. Why did humans cling to life so tenaciously when *this* was how they lived?

A hallway lay before me with two doors leading off it—bedrooms, I assumed—and opened into a kitchen at the back of the house. To my left, beyond an arched doorway, was a home office with an overburdened desk and a wall of bookshelves.

Something bumped my ankle, and I jumped.

A massive ball of white fluff meowed and rubbed against my leg. Frank's cat. I chuckled at my apprehension.

"What's your name, little one?" I knelt and fingered its pink collar. A purr vibrated my hand as I read its tag. Diana. Named for the Roman goddess of the hunt. How fitting.

Diana's green-eyed gaze met mine, and her purr cut off abruptly. Her ears twitched back, and her eyes narrowed. She'd seen my soul.

The eyes are the windows of the soul. Cats have always been peeping toms, though they have no immortal souls of their own. Diana didn't hiss but rather sniffed my hand as though confirming her suspicions.

"Yes, Diana. It is I, the Grim Reaper, terror of men's souls. But I don't scare you, do I? Your master trapped me in his body and ran off with my scythe and cowl. I don't suppose you know where he keeps his spell books?"

Diana's tail twitched, and she padded across the living room. I followed, curious.

Cats have always fascinated me. They have a species memory of being worshiped as gods. Of ancient times when demons and angels with delusions of grandeur used cats as their chosen vessels. Cat possession fell out of vogue among spirit-kind several thousand years ago, but cats as a species retained the skills imparted upon them by the spirits. They could see angels and demons, and they transited realms at will.

I doubt humans would be so quick to invite cats into their homes if they knew that little tidbit of information. That Fluffy wasn't just hiding under the couch, but was visiting fiends in the Realm of Torments, looking for servants to show them proper obeisance.

Diana led me into the kitchen and sat, staring intently at a cupboard. I opened the door with a creak. A bag of kitty kibble flopped to the tile floor. I jumped back and tiny brown pebbles skittered in a fan around Diana, who'd placed herself perfectly to receive the brunt of the avalanche. Her tail twitched, and she settled in to eat. My eyes narrowed.

She'd set me up. Diana didn't care about my existential crisis. She just wanted dinner.

I pursed my lips and left her to it. Where best to start my search? I doubted Frank kept his spell books in the kitchen, so I trudged back down the hall.

The living room revealed nothing of interest. Nor did the bedroom or Frank's home office. Well, the office was *interesting,* just not in the way I'd hoped. The wall of bookshelves overflowed with occult and religious texts. I scanned the titles. Plenty about the afterlife and Yours Truly, but nothing ancient. No Sumerian soul spells, just an unhealthy fascination with death.

No surprise there.

I paused at a bulletin board tacked with thank you notes from lawyers and CPAs, gratitude for Frank helping their clients clear debt and acquire refunds. Odd. I wouldn't have expected such helpful behavior from an auditor.

Back in the kitchen, I stepped around Diana and her feast and tried two doors in the corner. One led to an empty garage—I'd left Frank's car at work—and the other opened to an unfinished stairwell. I descended into darkness.

Chapter 3

BONE DUST

DARKNESS ENGULFED ME AS I descended the creaky wooden staircase into the center of Frank's unfinished basement. The hair on the back of my neck stood up, and I grimaced. Fear was irrational, a human response to dark spaces and the unknown terrors that lurked there. Regardless, my steps slowed. Stale, moist air greeted me, and wood creaked underfoot, echoing in the darkness. My heart quickened of its own accord. My hand brushed against a light switch.

A bulb flickered on, revealing the logical result of Frank's occult research. Painted archaic symbols covered the empty cement floor, each with unlit candles at intersection points. Summoning circles from different civilizations.

Bingo.

Nothing to fear here unless I was a summoned spirit. Among the circles, I recognized Babylonian, Greek, Chinese, Egyptian, and—ah-ha!—Sumerian. That one had intricately woven runes surrounding charred cement and feathery ash.

I circled the dank room, stepping around the summoning circles, examining each. It was a testament to mankind's tenacity that every civilization devised methods of controlling spirits. Tucked under the open stairs was Frank's workspace—a tattered recliner beside a rickety apothecary cabinet filled with papers, moldering books, and scrolls. Artifacts in labeled jars and little plastic baggies filled the apothecary cabinet's little cubby holes.

I examined Frank's prizes. Newt eyes, bat wings, spices, poisons, and more. Stickers decorated many with RARE FIND!—CORDELIA'S APOTHECARY SUPPLY.

I arched an eyebrow. Cordelia? She was a tax auditor *and* an apothecary? Interesting.

I retrieved a rolled-up bundle of copy paper jammed

between the legs of a stuffed crow. My breath caught. Pictures of ancient Sumerian tablets filled the top page with hand-written translations scrawled along the edges. The papers crinkled in my grip. This was it.

I drew a deep breath, smoothed out the papers, and read. I wasn't limited by human language barriers, so translation wasn't a problem.

The content was.

There was nothing here about swapping souls. It was a simple summoning spell.

I dropped into the recliner with a huff and read through again. Nothing. I scratched my jaw. Frank's beard was soft under my fingertips. Everything about Frank seemed soft. Slovenly. Yet he'd been oddly methodical in his quest to swap our souls. His library upstairs attested to years of research. So where had he gotten the Sumerian spell?

I considered the summoning circles. Perhaps he'd summoned a demon and gotten the spell from *them*. I eyed the apothecary cabinet's little cubby holes. The stuffed crow eyed me back.

Follow Frank's steps. Summon a demon, then ask it about the spell. I nodded to myself, jumped up, and set to work.

Fifteen minutes later the Sumerian circle was set up with candles, cinnamon, and bone dust from a Sumerian priest—if the baggie label was to be believed. I turned off the light and stood at the circle's edge. My grip tightened on Frank's ceremonial dagger. I'd never performed a summoning spell before. What if I got it wrong?

Heavens, what if I got it right? Who would come? The Auditor? Beelzebub? Lucifer himself? No, not Lucifer. The Lord of Darkness was too powerful for a mere summoning, he'd send a minion. But who? The not-knowing gnawed at me.

I drew a deep breath and blew it out.

Indecision was only letting the candles burn down. Waiting wasn't solving anything. I chanted the incantation seven times. A quick prick of a finger held over the circle, and then I snatched my hand back before the blood landed.

Good thing.

A bolt of red lightning arced up when my blood struck the cement. It bounced off the circle's invisible walls, splitting and multiplying until an inferno of crackling red electricity connected cement to bare joists. My skin tingled and my hair stood on end before the entire light show condensed into a single bolt again. It struck the center of the circle with a hellish boom that rattled the stairs. Lava bubbled through the cement and from that rose a demon's hideous form, clad in a wrinkled gray suit.

He stood only two feet tall.

I smiled, the knot in my chest easing somewhat. It was Alvin, recently promoted head of Bureaucratic Torments. Not a friend, really, but our paths had crossed. Horns poked through his thin, greasy comb-over, and his sharp red eyes glared at me. He pointed a clawed finger. His voice sounded like a strangled weasel.

"That's it, Frank! I'm sending my cousin Brutus to make your life a living hell until the *day … you … die!* Then, when your soul finds its way to Hell, I'm gonna—"

"I am not Frank Totmann," I said, and Alvin paused, his angry glower turning to confusion. He focused on my eyes then gasped.

"In the name of Lucifer," he whispered, "he did it." Alvin's brows scrunched. "Oh, Grim. How you doing?"

Heat surged through my chest, and my breath came short and fast. "You … you knew?" I stepped forward, fists clenched, breaking the circle with a flash of red electricity. "You *knew* Frank Totmann's plan and didn't *think* to warn me? He stole my scythe! My power! My very identity!" My hand shot toward Alvin's throat, but he leapt back.

"It wasn't like that!" His hands flew up, warding me off as I stalked forward. "Frank's daily summonings were annoying the crap out of me. I had to give him something, so I found a soul transfer spell he couldn't use. The ingredients were impossible to acquire!" Alvin slid under the open stairs between the recliner and the apothecary cabinet.

"Impossible? Look at me! I'm stuck in a human body thanks to *you*!" I slapped the stairs as I ducked under them. Dust shook loose and the *crack* of my hand on the wood echoed off empty cement walls.

Alvin flinched and dodged back around the Egyptian circle. "The spell required the bones of a Sumerian priest!"

"You idiot!" I spun toward the apothecary, snatched a labeled baggie, and read it aloud. "Sumerian Priest Bone Dust." I threw the bag at Alvin. It passed through his chest and slid across the floor. "That was a basic ingredient of his summoning circle!"

Alvin raised a finger to protest, but his words died unspoken. His finger lowered slowly. "Oh. Uh, sorry."

My anger flared hot before draining away. I sat heavily

on the stairs and dropped my head into my hands. "Me too. More than you could possibly imagine." I drew a shuddering breath then looked up. "Was there a reversal on that Sumerian spell?"

"How should I know?" Alvin's flippancy brought me to my feet, fists clenched again. He raised placating hands. "But I can check."

I drew deep, calming breaths. Death was supposed to be emotionless. Impartial. The first time I got angry, *really* angry, had been over something stupid. An argument with the Auditor about sins and sacrifices. I'd been an angel then. So young. I tried to prove my point about innate human goodness, whispered a lie into Cain's ear, and accidentally incited him to murder Abel.

Humanity's first death. Their first murder. Heaven had still been reeling with the aftershocks of Lucifer's betrayal and dropped me into Purgatory to await Judgment. To avoid eternal torment, I begged Gabriel for clemency. I could atone for my crime by easing mankind's souls into the next world.

He bought it and I sidestepped Judgment, which really pissed off the Auditor. He'd been angling for the job.

Lucifer offered to forge my scythe when he heard what

had happened and presented it to the Almighty for blessing; a peace offering between realms. They named it *Grace*. A blade to impart balance, to winnow souls with minimal fuss. "For by *Grace* you have been saved," the Almighty had intoned with satisfaction. Lucifer had rolled his eyes and mumbled something about a coup de grâce as he shoved the scythe into my hands.

Thus was the Grim Reaper born. No longer an angel, not quite a demon, bound to serve both Heaven and Hell and beholden to neither. All because of my rash anger.

My pocket vibrated with a cheerful ring, and I jumped. I dug out Frank's phone and read the message on the screen.

Cora: *I'm at Edelweiss! You on your way?*

Alvin stepped around to peer at the screen. "You old dog," he said, turning corporeal and punching my shoulder. "One day as a human, and you've already got a date!"

I rose, shielding the phone from his view. "Frank had dinner plans before he died. Well, almost died. There is no need to maintain his schedule." My stomach twitched and gurgled with unfamiliar pain.

Alvin looked at my belly, then the phone, and chuckled. "You're human now, subject to four incessant needs."

I raised an imperious eyebrow at the dirty-minded

cretin. "Implying what?"

Alvin barked a laugh. "No, Grim, not sex. That's necessary for species survival, not the individual. No, you'll need an appalling amount of food, water, and sleep to keep that body functional." He made a shooing gesture. "Go. Go on your date. I'll see what I can find about reversing that spell."

I nodded and said, "Thank you." Perhaps Cora could provide insights into the spell as well. She *had* provided the ingredients.

Alvin retrieved the baggie of Sumerian Priest Bone Dust and then scuffed his clawed feet around the Sumerian summoning circle. White chalk, cinnamon, and bone dust smeared across the cement.

"What are you doing?" I asked.

"I'm done being summoned." Alvin finished destroying the circle and glanced around. He snatched the instructions from where I'd dropped them on Frank's recliner. Papers and baggie disappeared inside Alvin's rumpled suit jacket, creating a bulge. He nodded in satisfaction, gave me a double thumbs-up, and sank into the floor without the dramatic flair of his entrance.

"Wait!" I said. "You said humans have four incessant

needs. Hunger, thirst, sleep, and…?"

Alvin's descent paused at neck level, and his face split into a broad smile. "Pooping, my friend. What goes in must come out. A serious design flaw if you ask me. Good luck!" He waved cheerfully and disappeared.

My breath whooshed out, and I dropped back onto the stairs, making them groan. I often reaped souls from compromising positions, so I had a vague idea of what was coming, but I had never considered the mechanics of … defecation. My mind skittered around, refusing to focus. My gut rumbled, and I realized that I was, indeed, hungry.

Well, best get on with it. I retrieved Louis's card.

Chapter 4

GRIM ADVICE

MY SECOND RIDE IN Louis's cab was more terrifying than the first. The night was heavy and as dark as Abaddon. Headlights and streetlamps flashed past, creating snapshots of perceived surroundings before darkness settled again. It had taken me ten minutes of jabbing and swiping at Frank's phone before I figured out how to call the cabbie. A call that I was beginning to regret, but how else was I supposed to get around town? I couldn't drive myself.

My eyes were continually drawn back to the wildly swaying cardboard apple tree under Louis's mirror as he navigated curves at speed. I braced my feet in the footwell to avoid sliding across the cracked leather seat. The scent of artificial cleaners seemed stronger than before.

Louis glanced into the mirror. "Edelweiss is a nice restaurant. You got a hot date?"

I supposed that 'hot date' was one possible description of my pending dinner with Cora. I nodded. "I'll admit to being nervous." That was an understatement. "Any advice?"

Louis barked a sharp laugh. "Brother, you're asking the wrong guy for relationship advice. Nicole, my wife, is so pissed at me right now that I've been sleeping on the couch for a week!" He slammed on the brakes for a stop sign but barely paused before roaring through the intersection.

"What happened?" I asked.

"I, uh, forgot our anniversary."

"And that landed you on the couch?"

"Partly. I also bought her a vacuum."

"I don't understand."

A horn blared as Louis merged onto a thoroughfare, but I doubt he even noticed. At least the broad avenue was better lit than the side streets of Frank's neighborhood. "Nicole had been eying this thousand-dollar vacuum for months now," he said. "A Dyson Model X. It's the Cadillac of vacuums! Self-propelled, deep cleaning, and light as a feather. Best on the market, but a thousand bucks is a lot of money!" He sighed dramatically. "But I knew how much she wanted it. So, I quietly saved up, worked extra shifts, cut back on expenses, and bought it for her. Just my damned luck that I brought it home on our anniversary ... which I'd forgotten."

I frowned. "I feel like I'm missing the point here. You bought an expensive gift and presented it on your anniversary. How is that a bad thing?"

Louis rolled his eyes with a wry expression as he wove between two cars and turned onto another dark side street. "Apparently gifting a vacuum on your anniversary tells your wife she's nothing more than the hired help, not your partner. At least, that's what she yelled at me."

"Ah, I see. Did you apologize?"

"Hell, no! That thing was expensive! At this point, I'm as pissed at her as she is at me."

The cab tilted precipitously as Louis navigated a traffic circle without slowing. My heart lurched into my throat. I forced my death grip on the door to loosen. I'd read Louis's soul and he wasn't dying for another seven years. By extension, I should be perfectly safe, right?

Yeah, right.

Frank's cell phone rang, and I dug it out of my pocket. Cora probably wanted to confirm I was still coming.

"Hello? Cora?"

A mechanical voice answered. "Hi, I've been trying to reach you about your car's extended warranty."

I eyed the phone, then put it back to my ear. "Are you sure? This is the first call I've received." My brow furrowed. Taking over Frank's life was getting complicated. First the date with Cora, and now this?

"Well, I'm glad I reached you!" the mechanical caller said. "Today only, we have a special deal to extend your warranty for the low, low price of two-hundred dollars a month."

"That seems expensive."

"You can't put a price tag on peace of mind!"

"Pardon me, but what exactly is an extended warranty?"

Louis barked a laugh, and I met his gaze in the mirror. "You actually talk to those scam artists?" he said. "Hang up and save yourself a headache."

I eyed the phone again. The caller's mechanical voice became a muted babble as I pulled it from my ear. Scam artist? I was unfamiliar with the term but extrapolated its meaning. With a frown, I hung up as Louis screeched around a corner. We rocked to a stop outside Edelweiss Restaurant.

I paid him and climbed from the cab. My knees decided they weren't done being terrified from the ride and tried to buckle. I leaned on the open door, willing stability into my legs, and turned back to meet Louis's gaze. His few remaining years shone in those bright gray eyes.

"Do you love Nicole?" I asked. He nodded. "Life is too short to hold grudges. I suspect that if you apologized, Nicole might rescind your couch banishment."

Louis blew out a heavy breath. "I know, but a man's gotta have his pride."

"Would you rather have pride with turmoil or peace with humility?"

"Hmmm..." Louis nodded. "I'll think on it. Enjoy your date, Grim!" He waved. I closed the door and eyed the restaurant as Louis zoomed away.

Cora was in there, waiting for me. Well, waiting for Frank, but I had to pretend. Somehow. How was I going to fake my way through a date? I couldn't lie.

Focus, Grim. This wasn't a date; it was an opportunity to interrogate Cora. She helped Frank with ingredients for his Sumerian spell. Surely, she knew something that could help me reverse it.

I could only hope.

Chapter 5

JÄGERSCHNITZEL

EDELWEISS RESTAURANT LOOKED WARM and inviting, a beacon of tranquility on a cold night. Low eaves were lined with warm track lighting which gave the heavy stone columns and shake siding a pleasant old-world glow. The hum of conversation drifted from outdoor seating to the left, and a whiff of something rich and decadent made my stomach rumble. Dishes clanked and propane heaters glowed red as jacketed diners enjoyed fall's dying warmth. I shivered in Frank's tweed suit and hoped Cora's table was inside. I headed for the door.

Sharp pain sliced through my chest, arcing into my left

shoulder. I gasped and dropped onto a wooden bench. It felt like an elephant had just stomped on my chest. My heart raced, paused, then raced again. I gasped, struggling to stay upright. I clutched the bench's aged rail. Splinters stabbed my palm.

Frank's heart gave four more syncopated beats before settling down. I drew deep breaths and massaged my chest. This heart was past its expiration date. It wouldn't last much longer.

A young man inside escorted me to a corner booth in a room topped with faux roof eaves. Blue and white checkered bunting, a cloud-painted ceiling, and rough wooden panels gave the impression of outdoor dining without the chill Colorado winds. The restaurant's busy clatter filled the dining room. Cora beamed when she saw me.

"Hey, there. I was worried you'd stand me up."

"I apologize for my tardiness. I usually make a point of arriving just when people need me." What would happen to a soul if I didn't arrive on time? Would the body die and decay with the soul trapped inside? I'd seen something similar once, and I never wanted to see it again. Yet, would that be my fate if I died? Disturbed by my thoughts, I slid into the booth.

Cora said, "I ordered for us. You're going to *love* the Jägerschnitzel."

As if on cue, a waiter arrived with plates. I eyed mine with trepidation. Everything was a uniform brown. Breaded meat was buried under thick mushroom gravy, and piled French fries threatened to topple off the plate. The fries were sprinkled with a red powder which added a spicy kick to the greasy scents wafting upward.

It smelled fantastic. My stomach agreed with loud gurgles.

I glanced at Cora, but she had already dug in. New to the intricacies of eating, I copied what she did. The silverware was tricky, but I managed my first bite.

Greasy bliss melted on my tongue. I closed my eyes, and a groan escaped as I chewed and swallowed.

"See, told you it was good."

I gazed into Cora's smiling eyes. "That was ... amazing." I cut another bite. "Is all food this good?" No wonder humans spent so much of their lives eating. That bite followed the first, and I groaned again as she nodded.

"Here? Most of it. If you have room for dessert, their Apfelstrudel is to die for."

"To die for?" A third and fourth bite disappeared. "I'll

take the chance."

Cora chuckled, a warm sound that revealed her bright soul.

The waiter brought us beers that looked like bubbly swamp water. I took one sip and almost gagged. It tasted like swamp water too, but I was thirsty. I forced down a large draught.

Cora seemed content to talk about herself and her grown kids as we ate. One at college, another just having her first child. But a cloud passed over Cora's expression when she spoke of her youngest, Abigail.

"She'd just graduated college when she died. I miss her terribly." Her voice cracked, and she dug a heavy iron cross from among her many necklaces. It looked old, ancient even, and was engraved with Celtic runes. Like a misplaced holy relic. "This was Abigail's," she said. "I keep it close to remember her."

I swallowed my bite. "What happened?"

"It was that flash flood up in Manitou Springs two years back. Took two days to dig her car out of the mud."

I nodded, remembering. Five had died that day. Four had given the usual complaints about dying too soon, but not Abigail. She'd just nodded at me like an old friend and asked where she was going. Very direct, like her mother.

Cora wiped her eyes and smiled. "Look at me, being maudlin on a date. Sorry."

"Loss is hard. We all cope differently." When I'd lost Evelyn, the only one I ever cared about, I'd buried myself in work. That had filled my time but failed to assuage my guilt. Evelyn's face continued to haunt me, despite the millennia.

I gave myself a shake. I wasn't here to talk about my failures. "Was that when you began your apothecary business?" I reached for my beer and realized it was empty. The waiter signaled that he'd bring another.

A renewed smile lit Cora's face. It was the look of an enthusiast asked to speak on their favorite topic. "I'd dabbled on the fringes of the dark arts for years before Abigail's death, much to my children's annoyance. But yes, Cordelia's Apothecary Supply went online not long after I lost her. Now, business is booming. Soon, I may be able to retire from the IRS and work it full-time! That's the dream anyway."

"Where do you acquire your artifacts?" I asked as a beer appeared at my elbow. I took another long pull. It still tasted bitter, but went down smoothly, lubricated by its predecessor.

"That's the joy of the internet. You can find anything if you dig hard enough."

Like a soul-swapping spell reversal?

The waiter derailed my line of questioning with dessert. Decimated dinner plates disappeared and were replaced with a fluffy pastry that oozed baked apples and cinnamon. Apfelstrudel, I assumed. Pillowy vanilla ice cream lay atop a flaky crust, melting in thin streams. It smelled divine.

I took a large bite and Cora asked, "So what are your dreams?"

"Hmmph?" I mumbled around the glorious blending of hot, cold, and sweet.

"Nobody wants to be a tax auditor when they grow up. What else do you want?"

I swallowed and sat back. What did *I* want? Nobody had asked me that before. I searched my soul. "I like my job, helping souls in need. I'm good at it, but it gets lonely."

Cora gripped my hand, her bracelets jangling. "You're not alone anymore." She quirked a smile. "Did you know that the girls at the office tried to warn me off? Said that a confirmed bachelor must have deep, dark secrets." She released my hand, leaving a ghost of warmth on my skin.

"I'm glad I didn't listen. You're really quite sweet."

The rest of dinner passed in a pleasant blur. My thoughts turned sluggish by the end, victims of the food and drink. When we rose to leave, I stumbled and caught myself on the wall. The restaurant blurred around me, and it was only with sheer willpower that I made my eyes focus.

What was wrong with me? Was it another heart attack? I didn't feel any pain. Rather, my chest and head felt light and fluffy. Like that marvelous dessert.

Cora cocked an eyebrow and took my elbow. "Looks like I'm driving you home."

"Pardon?"

"You went after that beer like a parched man in the desert."

"I was thirshty." I scowled at the slurred words and focused. "Thirsty." My thoughts tried to race, failed miserably, and my scowl deepened as realization slowly dawned on me. I wasn't dying. I was drunk! How could I have been so careless? I glanced at Cora's beer. Still half-full. She'd shown more restraint than I had. "Apologies. I've made a fool of myshelf … myself."

"Don't worry about it! I'll finally get to see that bachelor pad of yours and"—she smiled slyly—"meet the other woman in your life."

"What?" Other woman? What kind of a cad was Frank Totmann? Dating the charming Cordelia while he lived with someone else? How dare he! I tried to pull away, but Cora chuckled and guided me toward the exit.

"Diana, silly. Your cat?"

Oh. Right. I bit my tongue—a painful idiom when applied literally—and let her guide me outside to her Peugeot.

Cora's driving was much more pleasant than Louis's. The gentle vibrations of engine and road blended with her voice as she asked for directions. My eyes slid shut. It had been a very long day.

Sleep came unbidden and wrapped me in velvet arms as I succumbed to Alvin's third incessant need.

Chapter 6

INCESSANT NEEDS

TUESDAY MORNING BROUGHT CONFUSION and the overwhelming scent of Cora's lotus flower perfume. I woke in an ocean of downy blankets and soft pillows as sunlight pierced a nearby window. A small desk sat below the window; neat and orderly with a stool tucked beneath it. Flowered wallpaper and framed photos surrounded me. Smiling portraits of unknown children interspersed with candid photos of a life well-lived.

This was not Frank's bedroom.

I sat bolt upright in bed. A pounding sensation like a tiny man with an anvil thumped at the base of my skull.

Heavens above! I'd heard of hangovers, but descriptions paled in comparison to the reality.

I put a hand to the back of my neck, and the blankets dropped away, revealing plaid boxers and a white tank top that covered a mat of wiry body hair. It was like Frank's hair had abandoned his head and taken up residence on his chest. I wasn't naked, but I felt exposed. My gaze whipped around the room. There, neatly folded on a stool under the desk, were my clothes, shoes set on the carpet beside the desk.

I swung my legs off the bed and stood. Plush carpeting squished softly between my toes. A yawn cracked my jaws, and my body insisted on stretching, arms and shoulders back. It was an awkward motion that dropped me onto the bed again. I landed and abruptly realized that I had bigger problems than my state of undress or even my headache. Intense pressure on my bowels screamed for attention.

Alvin's fourth incessant need had found me.

I scrambled for my pants. I had one leg on and was struggling with the other when a light knock on the door made me freeze. The door swung open, and Cora swept in, two steaming mugs clutched by their handles in one hand. Her flowered bathrobe matched the wallpaper.

I tried to shove my foot through the pantleg, but my toes caught. I overbalanced and hit the floor with a grunt. Cora chuckled as I finally managed to get the pants over my hips.

"You weren't nearly this shy last night."

I goggled at her and rose. The pants slid down, and I yanked them back up. The boxers bunched around my hips. I clutched at my belt and tried to remember the previous night. Flashes came, clouded and disjointed. Cora had walked me to this room, helped me hang my jacket behind the door, and then ... nothing.

"I ... um..."

Cora chortled, her face simply beaming at my discomfiture. "I'm sorry, I shouldn't tease. Nothing happened. You were a perfect gentleman, which I appreciate. Not many of those around these days. You fell asleep in the car, and I brought you here instead of hunting for your house." She proffered a mug. "Coffee?"

The pressure on my bowels intensified, and I grimaced. My cheeks warmed with embarrassment. "Forgive me, but ... um, where is your toilet?"

Her eyebrows shot up. "Oh, right. End of the hall. I'll, uh, meet you downstairs." She stepped aside, and I bolted past her.

At the end of the hall, I found the toilet and slammed the door. There was a bit of fumbling before, to my ever-lasting horror, I discovered the heinous reality of defecation. Mortality's dark side. It was noisy, putrid, and mortifying.

Humans do this every day? I would rather die.

I flushed, scrubbed my hands as if cleaning the stain off my soul, and fled the smelly little room.

I took the time to carefully reassemble my wardrobe before heading downstairs. My headache had dimmed, and I followed my nose to the kitchen.

It was a perfectly square room lined with cupboards, a refrigerator on the far wall and a stove to the right. Cora hovered over the stove, whistling as she scrambled eggs with a spatula in one hand, a white floral oven-mitt on the other. I sat in a breakfast nook to the left of the refrigerator, in front of two narrow windows that bracketed the corner of the room. Through the windows I saw the neighbor's wooden fence mere feet away. Morning sunlight warmed my face. The coffee Cora had tried to give me earlier sat on the table. I took a sip.

A toaster popped. My stomach rumbled with Alvin's first incessant need at the rich aroma of breakfast. I drummed my fingers on the table, unsure what to do. What to say. Cora glanced over her shoulder and saved me the trouble.

"So, how's your little project going?"

Project? What project? "Well, you know how these things happen. Ups and downs." I smiled to myself, pleased at my vagueness. I was getting the hang of talking around my inability to lie.

"Did that Sumerian priest's bone dust work?"

"Perfectly," I said then snapped my jaw shut. Fool!

Cora spun, spatula in hand. "It worked? Really? What happened? I want every detail!" Egg fell from the utensil and splattered on the floor.

I blinked at her. If she knew about Frank's plans to cheat Death, to swap our places, then ... "You know that I'm not Frank?"

Cora's eyes bulged. "What?" She backed against the stove; spatula suddenly remembered. She brandished it like a sword.

Damn. I ran a hand through Frank's thin hair. "You were speaking of summoning the demon, weren't you?"

She nodded, eyes wide. Her voice rose in tone and volume. "Are you the demon? Where's Frank? What did you do to Frank?!"

"It's more like 'what did Frank do to me?'" I rose, anger making my tone dark and sharp.

Cora pressed herself back. The pan scraped across the stovetop behind her. "Stay back, demon!" She jabbed the spatula at me then spun and grabbed the pan in her mitted hand. She whipped it around like a cast-iron shield between us. Half-cooked eggs flew, and I tried to duck. I was too slow.

My jaw clenched, and I wiped egg from my face. "I am *not* a demon. I am the Grim Reaper, trapped in Frank's failing mortal coil."

All color drained from Cora's face. "Oh, God. You killed Frank."

"No, that conniving auditor cheated *me*. *Death!* He stole my scythe, my cowl, my identity—everything! And now he's running around doing Heaven-knows-what while I fumble around trying to be human!"

Cora's jaw worked for a moment before she said, "I'm sorry. Run that by me again?"

"Your boyfriend used the ingredients that *you* provided to swap souls with me. I need to reverse his spell before..." I clamped my jaw shut. She didn't need to know about the

Auditor. No need to scare her further. "I need your help."

"He planned this?"

"To the last detail."

Cora's jaw clenched. Tears brimmed in her eyes, and she muttered to herself, "And he didn't say a thing to me. Asshole."

"Then you'll help me?" I stepped forward.

Cora brandished the pan. Her eyes narrowed. "No."

"But—"

"You took my Abigail before her time. I still wake up some days thinking she's alive, sleeping in the next room. And then I remember. Do you know what that's like? The crushing weight of loss? Of grief?"

My thoughts jumped to Evelyn. To the way her chestnut eyes had smiled whenever she looked at me. Yes, I understood grief. Even after five thousand years. I swallowed the lump in my throat and tried to interrupt, but Cora's anger rolled over my words. She jabbed the pan at me accusingly.

"Everybody dies. I know that. But Death should visit us in old age, after a long and fulfilling life. Not a girl just beginning her life, full of hope and promise." Tears were flowing freely now, and Cora stalked forward, heedless of the scrambled eggs she stepped through. "She was my favorite, you know. Parents aren't supposed to have favorite children, but I did. Abigail was one in a million, and *you* took her from me!"

She jabbed the pan into my chest, and I dropped into the chair. Heat wafted from the pan, and Cora loomed over me, a mother's righteous fury burning in her eyes. "I will never help Death take my loved ones away."

"You don't understand. There is more at stake here—"

She slammed the pan onto the table, and I jumped. "Never! I'm glad that Frank cheated Death. Cheated *you*."

Silence spread between us, and I stared into Cora's eyes. I saw truth there. She meant every word. Anger, sorrow, and determination warred across her face. Finally, determination won, and she straightened.

"I'll take you back to the office, but then you're on your own."

"The office? What would *I* do at the Land of Evil Auditors?"

Cora's expression was grim but satisfied. "You'll learn what it means to be human."

"Meaning what?"

"Meaning that life is hard, but it's worth living. We work, struggle, survive, and thrive. We fight every day to keep Death at bay. To truly live while we're still alive."

I didn't have answer for that.

Cora spun on her heel and stomped back to the stove. The rattle when she slammed down the cast-iron pan could have woken the dead. She turned the stove off, threw her flowered oven mitt onto the counter, and stormed from the room. Over her shoulder, she shouted, "I'm taking a shower. We'll leave in fifteen minutes. Be ready."

I slumped back into the chair. Great. Just great. I'd alienated my only ally, and now she was throwing me to the wolves.

No, worse than wolves. She was throwing me to the auditors.

Chapter 7

THE LOGISTICIAN

IT TOOK CLOSER TO an hour before Cora was ready, but I felt it wisest not to comment. As she descended the stairs, the fire in her eyes dared me to say something. Anything.

I bit my tongue, though not literally. I'd learned from last time.

The drive to the Land of Evil Auditors was quiet and tense. I scratched at Frank's beard, which was starting to itch. After a silent fifteen-minute drive that felt like fifteen hours, we reached the expansive parking lot. We exited the vehicle and Cora stomped toward the building while I plodded silently behind her.

It was another clear day in Colorado Springs. As clear and cold as the anger wafting off Cora. The blue sky was framed by the stark ridgeline with just a few brush-stroke-thin clouds that stretched from horizon to horizon. A flying V of geese passed low overhead, honking their displeasure as they fled to warmer climes. If only I could escape so easily.

I didn't want to take over Frank's life and job, but I didn't see any other options. I needed to pass for human long enough for Alvin to find that spell reversal. I've never known a more capable bureaucrat, so it was just a matter of time before he got back to me. But until he did, I had to pretend to be an auditor for the Internal Revenue Service. An *auditor*.

Heaven help me.

Cora reached the building's glass front door before I did and swept through. The door slammed in my face. I paused, lips pursed.

Okay, I get it. Cora wasn't my biggest fan, but that was no reason to be rude. Through the door I watched her follow a black runner carpet to the right to join two men waiting for the elevator. One of them said something, and she laughed as though she hadn't a care in the world.

I gripped the door handle, and my eyes narrowed. How could Cora go from angry to happy so fast? She glanced back at me, and a cloud passed briefly over her expression before she replied to her companion with that beaming smile.

Oh, I see. She was pretending. I could do that. Pretending didn't require active lying. How hard could it be?

I swung the door open and tried to imitate Cora's confident swagger. It worked beautifully for the first three steps. Then I tripped on the runner carpet. I flailed and stumbled into the wall to my right, catching myself on a bulletin board bedecked with safety flyers.

"Rough morning, Frank?" one of the men asked as I righted myself.

"Like you couldn't imagine." I straightened my suit jacket as the elevator dinged open.

A tall, scrawny demon stepped out.

I froze. The demon wore the ubiquitous rumpled gray suit in vogue with Hell-spawn these days. A minion of Hell's Bureaucracy. Cora and the two men didn't see the demon, who in turn didn't bother to notice them. He stepped out of the elevator as they entered, his gaze locked on a small piece of yellow notepaper in his hand. I slowed, curious, as the elevator door slid closed.

The demon glanced up and scanned the entryway. His thin lips pursed. I followed his gaze but didn't see anything beyond a tan hallway leading to my left with brown linoleum floors and closed doors. The hall's bleak uniformity ended with a glass wall on the right side that said CAFÉ in bold letters. The demon glanced at his paper again, then spun toward a building directory near the stairwell, just past the elevator. He seemed completely oblivious to my presence.

What was a demon doing in the Land of Evil Auditors?

Okay, perhaps I answered my own question there, but *why* was he here? Was he a messenger? Had Alvin sent him with my spell reversal? Or was he a minion of the Auditor himself?

The demon consulted his yellow notepaper again, eyed the directory, then slid through the stairwell door.

Showoff. Memories of yesterday's encounter with the door made my jaw clench. I strode purposefully toward the stairwell and yanked the door open. The demon was already halfway toward the basement.

"Wait," I said, but he didn't turn or even slow. I scowled and followed as quickly as I could. By the time I reached the basement, he was halfway down a hall that ran the length of the building. He passed through an office door on the left.

The basement was musty but well-lit. The first half was sectioned supply cages while the far end was a standard hallway with two heavy doors. Twin signs dangled from pipes that ran the length of the ceiling. Logistics Department to the left. Information Technology to the right. The demon had gone left.

Odd.

IT departments were common entry points from the underworld. Why hadn't the demon simply entered the Land of Evil Auditors from there? And what business did he have with a logistician?

I strode past packed supply cages and stopped outside the Logistics Department. A plaque beside the door said, SAMUEL DAVIDSON. I glanced over my shoulder at the IT department.

A handwritten sign taped to the door announced that they were out to coffee. Hmmm... Perhaps the demon had knocked on a server door and nobody had answered.

A high-pitched scream erupted from Logistics Department, and I leapt back. It was the sound of a tormented soul. A scream of abject terror followed by indistinct blubbering for mercy.

Muscles tense, I swung the door open expecting to walk in on a murder scene. The room was lined with shelves full of office supplies, and a desk sat toward the back of the room. My attention, however, was arrested by the stand-off in the center of the room.

A middle-aged man in a blue-collared shirt and khakis stood between the demon and me, his back to the door. Samuel Davidson, I presumed. He brandished a short blade at the demon, whose eyes bulged. Clawed hands were raised high, and the scrap of paper fluttered toward the floor.

"Wait-wait-wait!" the demon was saying as it backed away. "We can make a deal. You do your job, I do mine, and nobody has to get banished!"

Samuel shook his head. "Begging? That's new. The last several demons were all bluster and intimidation. Not that it helped them in the end. Give my regards to Alvin Bureaucracy."

My eyebrows shot up. Samuel Davidson knew *Alvin?* Who was this man? And why was the demon afraid of him? Humans couldn't harm—

Samuel lunged forward and the small, thin blade slid into the demon's chest. There wasn't any blood or sparkly lights or anything so dramatic. The demon simply disappeared with a small *pop.*

My jaw dropped. Samuel Davidson had a blessed blade.

I'd heard of humans granted dispensation by Heaven to join in spiritual warfare, but I hadn't seen one in action since Joan of Arc. And with a genuine blessed blade! Which blade was it? It was too small to be Excalibur or Zulfiqar.

The door clicked shut behind me, and Samuel spun. He had a face that looked like it preferred smiling to frowning—despite its current intense expression—short brown hair, and intelligent brown eyes that showed me his soul. Samuel Davidson, forty-two years old, death in thirty-one years. His blade disappeared behind his back before I got a good look at it.

"Oh, hey Frank," he said, an easy smile appearing. "Didn't hear you there. How's it goin'?"

"You ... your blade..."

Samuel's lips pursed, but his tone remained light. "What, this thing?" He pulled the blade from behind his back. It was a miniature medieval sword no more than six inches in length that resembled none of the blessed blades I knew. Indeed, it looked rather cheap with its plain cross guard and clearly dull edges. "It's just a letter opener. Picked it up in Germany years ago on a layover. Adds that necessary barbarism when opening official correspondence." He held it out for inspection.

"But you were ... you just..."

A wry smile creased his face. "Ah, you caught me just playing around." He leaned forward and lowered his voice. "Don't tell anyone. It gets boring down here in the basement."

"You banish demons ... for fun?"

"What?" All amusement dropped from his face, and he straightened. "You saw the demon?"

Damn it! I needed to learn when to keep my big mouth shut! Well, in for a penny, in for a pound. I crossed my arms. "How do you know Alvin Bureaucracy?"

"Woah, slow down, buddy. Let's back up to the relevant point here. You can see demons?"

"Yes."

"Angels?"

"Of course."

"How long has your third eye been open?"

This was getting me nowhere. "I need to talk to Alvin Bureaucracy. He's looking into something to repay a favor he owes me."

The blade lowered to Samuel's side, his fingers flipping it into a fighting grip. It wasn't brandished at me, but the warning was clear. I needed to tread carefully.

"What do you need from Alvin?" he asked.

"Research."

"Into what?"

"Spell reversals."

Samuel's head cocked to one side. "Spells? As in ... magic? Are you telling me that magic is *real*?"

"You bear a blessed blade. What else would you call it?"

"Divine intervention in my time of need. I've had *Faith*"—he waggled the blade as he named it—"for years now. Good thing too because demons keep showing up in my office." He gestured to where the hapless minion had been moments before. "But you've avoided my question. I banished a demon in front of you two weeks ago, and you didn't bat an eye."

Because I wasn't here two weeks ago. That was the real Frank.

"I was rather proud of that banishment," he said. "Right

out in public. So, spill the beans, Frank. What happened?"

Could I trust him? He had connections to Alvin, which was a point in his favor, though I wasn't sure what that connection was since he'd just banished a demon. Yet I needed an ally, someone to help me traverse the confusing world of being human. I drew a deep breath.

"I am not Frank Totmann. I merely possess his body. Frank—"

"Demon!" Samuel's lip curled into a snarl. He brandished *Faith*, and I raised my hands.

"Not really. I am—"

He lunged, and I threw myself back against the door. He slashed, and I dodged to the left. My shoulder hit a metal supply shelf packed with cleaning supplies. Spray bottles rocked and tumbled free. I scrambled along the shelves, away from Samuel, dancing around the bottles as they bounced on the scuffed linoleum. Samuel followed like a stalking hunter, crouched with his ridiculous little letter opener held low in a white-knuckled grip. I didn't know what a blessed blade would do to me, but I didn't want to find out.

"Stop!" I said, reaching his desk at the back of the room. I stepped behind it and held out both hands. "Let me explain."

"Nothing to explain. I banish you and Frank gets his body back."

If only it were that easy.

Samuel lunged across the desk, stabbing at my chest. I slipped to the left and tried to bolt past him.

He was too fast. The stab turned into an awkward back-handed slash. The blade missed, but its handle snagged the collar of my tweed jacket. I yelped, tripped over my own feet, and fell into Samuel.

We crashed to the floor. For once Frank's bulk worked in my favor. I landed on top of Samuel, his arm trapped between us. His breath whooshed out in a grunt that smelled of day-old coffee. I scrambled up, and Samuel sucked air like a drowning man. *Faith* had clattered to the floor. I kicked it as I ran for the exit.

Sam rolled after the blade, and I slammed bodily into the door.

It didn't open. Damned door handles! I wrenched the handle, fell into the hall, and bolted for the stairwell. I crashed through that door and hit the stairwell at a dead run, sprinting up to the first landing. Laughing voices from above made me slow to an abrupt walk. A small crowd with coffee cups and pocket protectors filled the stairwell above me.

A fine time for IT to come to work! I squeezed past them, trying to control my breathing and my expression. Nothing to see here. Just a guy walking up the stairs.

My heart thundered in my chest, but I kept my measured pace to the main floor landing.

Which way? Sprinting up more stairs would likely make Frank's heart explode. There were two doors, one back to the building entryway and one leading outside, the same door I'd exited with Cora yesterday. Could I make it across the parking lot to the road?

No. Samuel was in better shape. He'd catch me in the open lot. I needed to hide and the only place I knew in the Land of Evil Auditors was Frank's office.

I popped through the interior door into the entryway. The elevator was open, employees piling in. I joined the crowd and squeezed in. Samuel Davidson strode into view as the doors slid together. He saw me, and his eyes narrowed. Then he was gone, lost behind the reflective steel doors that showed a dozen people all carefully not looking at each other. The floor shuddered beneath my feet, and the elevator rose.

I drew a deep breath. I'd escaped. For now.

"Hello ... Earth to Frank ... good morning," an elderly woman's sing-song voice said by my left elbow. I abruptly realized that she'd been talking since the moment I'd squeezed into the elevator. I gazed down at a cloud of blue-white hair framing a kindly face full of wrinkles. Heavy glasses made the woman's eyes look enormous, but I could still read her soul. Lucile Pembrook, eighty-nine years old. Death in four days.

"Um, good morning?" I didn't intend for it to sound like a question, but apparently the human brain doesn't flip easily from terrified flight to trivial small talk. She grinned, shoving wrinkles up under her glasses.

"Any morning this side of the grave is a good one in my book. What's got you so distracted?"

A husky woman's voice answered from the back corner of the elevator. "Frank and Cora had a date last night. Judging from Frank's dazed look, I think it went well." There was a distinct smirk in that voice. I craned my head toward the speaker but couldn't identify her among the crowd.

The young man next to me glanced over and wrinkled his nose. "Man, your breath stinks! Forget to pack your toothbrush in your overnight bag?" Chuckles filled the tight space and heat flushed my cheeks.

"I did not ... we didn't ... it was just dinner!" I realized that I was babbling, and I snapped my teeth shut with a click. The chuckles turned into full laughs, and I crossed my arms. My time with Cora was none of their business! The elevator opened on the third floor, and my departure was more hurried than dignified.

I paused after a few feet and eyed the cubicle farm, drawing deep, calming breaths. Cora's desk was forward left. I saw the top of her head, but she didn't see me. Two hallways extended from the far corners of the room. Frank's office was down the left one if memory served.

The stairwell door opened, and I glanced over my right shoulder.

Samuel Davidson locked eyes with me. He looked winded but determined. *He* didn't seem bothered by sprinting up the stairs. I didn't see *Faith*, his blessed letter opener.

I strode between the cubicles just fast enough that he'd have to run to catch me, but not so fast that I looked like I was fleeing for my life. I couldn't afford the attention of a public altercation. Nobody could know who I was. Both

Cora and Samuel had reacted ... poorly to the truth.

I glanced over my shoulder. Samuel paced me one aisle over, against the right-hand wall. I turned left at Cora's cubicle. She eyed me, jaw clenched, but said nothing. I reached the left-hand wall and almost ran over Lucile Pembrook.

I rocked to a stop lest I bowl over the little old lady. Lucile's brows rose in a questioning arch. "You haven't reviewed the Lisle audit yet. It was due yesterday." She held up a thick folder she hadn't had in the elevator. How had she managed to retrieve work from her desk and catch up with me in only a few seconds? Lucile was rather spry for an octogenarian with less than a week to live.

My lips pursed, and I heard Samuel's footsteps behind me. My shoulder blades itched, waiting for that blessed blade, but it didn't come. "Life took an unexpected turn yesterday," I told Lucile, "But my calendar is now free." I gestured toward the hallway and Frank's office. "Lead the way." And hurry!

She nodded and glanced past me with a cheerful, "Morning Sam! Need something?"

"Hey, Lucy," he said from right behind me. I could smell his coffee breath. "Just, uh, making my morning rounds.

Do *you* need anything?"

Lucile—no *Lucy*—smiled. And she'd called him Sam. I needed to start getting people's names right before they figured out that something was off. That I wasn't Frank Totmann. I sidestepped and turned so Sam wasn't behind me.

"I could use a hot date with a billionaire," she replied.

"Gold digger." Sam chuckled.

"You know it!" Lucy patted her hair and flashed Sam a smile that I supposed was meant to be sultry. "I need to finance my retirement!"

I snorted. Lucy wasn't headed for retirement with only four days remaining in this mortal coil. She caught my expression and punched my shoulder. Her knuckles were bony.

"Ow!"

"You think I can't catch a man?"

I rubbed my shoulder. "I do not doubt your determination to do whatever you want." Except survive until Saturday.

Lucy threw me a wink. "And don't you forget it!" She turned toward the hall, and I followed, listening for Sam's footsteps.

Silence. I glanced back.

Sam watched us go, a pensive look on his face. He was going to be a problem.

More pressing, however, was my pending meeting with Lucy. In about thirty seconds I needed to put on a dazzling song and dance to cover the fact that I knew absolutely nothing about audits.

My inability to lie was about to be taxed to its limit.

Chapter 8

MISTAKES AND MEMORIES

LUCY PRECEDED ME INTO Frank's office. She grabbed a chair from alongside the wall, then paused when she noticed the mess I'd left yesterday. Broken porcelain on the industrial carpet; spilled tea on the desk and floor. Papers had fallen from the desk and lay soaking in the remnants of Frank's magical concoction. The smell of anise and copper still lingered in the air.

"Really, Frank. How can you work in this kind of mess?"

"As I said, yesterday took an unexpected turn. I didn't have time to clean up." I made my voice stern. Frank was clearly in some sort of leadership position. Perhaps I could use that to avoid difficult questions.

Lucy's lips pursed, and she knelt to pick up shards of porcelain. Her knees cracked and her eyes tightened, but she didn't say anything. I retrieved the tea-soaked papers and the unbroken teacup which had rolled under the desk. Once everything was in a trash can, I dropped into Frank's chair with a sigh. I scratched my jaw. This beard really was getting quite itchy. Lucy perched on the edge of her chair and passed me the thick folder containing the Lisle audit.

I opened it with trepidation. Inexplicably complex forms greeted me. I flipped through pages, not understanding a word of it before leaning back.

"Why don't you give me a summary?"

Lucy nodded as if she'd been expecting the question. "This one's fairly straightforward. Sean Ruben Lisle, married filing jointly with Candice Josephina Lisle, owns and operates Lisle Electric. His wife is a nurse at Fred Wehling Memorial Hospital. However, both also work multiple part-time jobs which they failed to report, but their employers did. What tripped the audit, however, were business expenses far in excess of their claimed *and* unclaimed income."

"Hmmm," I said, trying to sound intelligent. "Why would a small business owner and a medical professional need to work additional jobs?"

Lucy's arched eyebrow said I'd asked the wrong question. "Don't know, but they owe $5,682 in additional taxes. It's summarized on page four of my report."

I flipped to page four. Numbers swam before my eyes as I tried to find something, *anything*, to comment on. What would Frank do? Was Frank the kind of supervisor who signed things without question, or would he dig further?

Despite his slovenly lifestyle, Frank had obsessively researched the occult until he found a way to cheat death. He would delve deeper.

I made a show of scanning the page. "They have a daughter, Gabriella," I said, grabbing at the only piece of information that might lead to a relevant question.

"Had. Gabriella was listed as deceased three years ago, the same tax year that I'm auditing."

Hmmm, Gabriella Lisle. I tried to remember...

Ah yes, she'd died of leukemia. She'd been a bright soul, cheerful despite her untimely demise, but worried about her parents. Something about medical bills. I set page four down and eyed Lucy.

"The Lisle family is working extra jobs to pay Gabriella's outstanding medical bills. She died of leukemia."

Lucy's brows furrowed. "How do you know…? Never mind. You always know more than you let on, though you could have told me. They didn't report medical expenses."

"Would that make a difference in your audit?"

"Of course! I'm not heartless. With an itemized Schedule A, deductible medical bills could easily eliminate any taxable income for the year."

I gestured to the phone on the desk. "Call them, see what you can work out."

Lucy flipped through the folder and found a number. When a woman answered, Lucy said, "Hello, Candice Lisle?"

"This is Nurse Lisle." Her voice was dim from the receiver against Lucy's ear.

"I'm Lucy Pembrook, the IRS auditor working on your case. Is this a good time?"

"Oh, uh, I'm at work, but…" She drew a deep breath. "Sure."

Lucy nodded. "Thanks. With me is Senior Auditor

Frank Totmann. We were reviewing your file and…"

I leaned back and crossed my arms. I didn't catch everything Candice Lisle said—

Wait, she'd called herself *Nurse* Lisle.

I didn't catch everything *Nurse* Lisle said, but her tone sounded tired and nervous. But then, who wouldn't be nervous with an auditor on their trail?

The call took several minutes, and Lucy shook her head after she'd disconnected. "They claimed the medical bills as business expenses." She rolled her eyes. "This is why people should just pay an Enrolled Agent or a CPA and not try doing taxes on their own! I'll do the Schedule A once Mrs. Lisle emails me Gabriella's medical bills. Poor woman."

I nodded in agreement, feeling rather good about myself. Perhaps being a tax auditor wasn't so hard. "There's always more to the story than what we see on the surface."

"True. I should have dug deeper." Lucy sat back in her chair, silent for a moment as she—I assume—considered the errors of her ways. Then she sat forward and rested her elbows on the desk, an amused gleam in her eye. "So, tell me about your date with Cora. How'd it go, really?"

I blinked at the abrupt topic shift. Why was everyone so

interested in my personal business?

"It went fine." No lie there. I just needed to avoid talking about breakfast this morning.

"Hmmm, I smell a story. Come on, Romeo, spill the gossip."

Ah, that was it. Lucy was the office gossip. I doubted she'd drop her line of questioning, so I outlined dinner as succinctly as possible. Good food, good conversation, end of story.

She smiled in a dreamy way when I finished. "Cora's a doll, you're lucky to have her."

"Indeed. It has been ... a long time since I've enjoyed another's company so. She was a breath of fresh air."

"Been out of the dating scene for a while?"

"I'd rather not say."

Lucy frowned at the warning tone in my voice. "I take it your previous relationship ended badly?"

I knew nothing of Frank's relationship history, but my own dark memories brought a heavy lump to my throat. Evelyn. Time may dull pain, but her face filled my mind's eye. Dark skin, piercing chestnut eyes, and wings blacker than the night sky. She'd been an angel of great beauty and martial renown, Gabriel's captain, and the only other soul

I've ever loved.

But she was gone now. Even after five millennia, remembering her fate made my gut churn. "It ended ... unexpectedly."

"She died?"

"No." My fingers drummed on the desk. How to explain this truthfully without *explaining* it? "We were working together on a large project of vast importance." Banishing demons and their half-human Nephilim and Demigod spawn to Abaddon, Hell's realm of eternal darkness. It had been before the Great Flood, but I remembered it like yesterday. "I was responsible for, uh, closing the deal"—my scythe *Grace* was and is the key to Abaddon—"while Evelyn dealt with the opposition." She'd commanded the Heavenly Host.

I could still smell the desert sands of Megiddo, pungent with the coppery tang of blood. Evelyn's scream at the end of the battle echoed in my ears. I saw her disappear, dragged into Abaddon by Nigel, King of the Demigods. Then Gabriel forced me to close the gates of Abaddon, sealing Hell's inescapable seventh level. Forever.

"Frank? Are you okay?" Lucy's concerned tone broke my reverie. I shook myself.

"Sorry, painful memories." I drew a shuddering breath. "The project was a success, a great victory proclaimed by all, but Evelyn paid the price for it. I never saw her after that."

Lucy's eyes narrowed. "You're not talking about tax audits, are you? Were you in the CIA or something?"

"I'd rather not talk about it at all."

She held up her hands. "Of course. Sorry. Prying into other people's business is what old ladies are good at." She smiled and pushed herself up. "I'll go see if Mrs. Lisle has sent those files. Perhaps you could tidy up a bit while I'm gone?" She eyed Frank's office with an arched eyebrow.

I nodded, not really listening. Lucy retrieved the Lisle file from my desk and then she was gone, leaving me alone with my memories, recriminations, and guilt.

I sat in silence for several minutes, but before the darkness overwhelmed me completely, I sprang to my feet, knocking Frank's chair back with squeaky protests. I couldn't fix the past, but I could fix the present. Control something in this insane cataclysm that humans called life.

Lucy was right. It was time to stop feeling sorry for myself and do something important. I couldn't solve my mortality problem right now, but there was something tangible I could do about the mess Frank had left me in.

I would clean his office.

Chapter 9

TORMENTS

IT TURNED OUT THAT cleaning was, indeed, good for distracting oneself from maudlin thoughts. I spent the morning puttering around Frank's office. Files went into drawers, surfaces were cleared, and the rubbish bin soon overflowed. I even found a yellowed plastic bottle of spray cleaner in the back of a cabinet. I doubted Frank put it there, he didn't seem the cleaning type, but by the time I finished, the surfaces shone like an ancient warrior's burnished bronze shield.

Dented and nicked bronze. Good enough. Satisfied with a job well done, I settled into Frank's chair and surveyed his tiny kingdom.

Now what?

My satisfaction dimmed when I realized that I'd just wasted hours I should have used trying to reverse Frank's soul-swapping spell. I'd been human for almost a full day and what did I have to show for it? A shiny desk.

Not that there was much else I could do. I was waiting for Alvin and his research. What was taking him so long? It had been—I glanced at the clock—eighteen hours since he'd promised to help. A bureaucrat of his prowess should have found my information long ago.

Frank's cell phone rang. I dug it out.

"Hello? Alvin?"

"Hi, I've been trying to reach you about your car's extended warranty." The mechanical voice was back. I frowned.

"I don't have a car." *Frank* had a car, but that was a technicality I could exploit. Telling the simple truth could work in my favor here.

"Our records indicate that your Honda Accord's warranty is about to expire and we're here to ensure that doesn't happen! With our extended warranty, you won't have to worry about—"

"I don't need an extended warranty." I wasn't going to be in this body long enough for it to matter.

"Everybody needs an extended warranty!"

"Do you have one?"

"Of course!"

"Liar! You're a machine!"

My mechanical caller ignored that. "Today only, we have a special deal to extend your warranty for the low, low price of two-hundred dollars a month."

"I'm not interested!" I said with finality and hung up.

I drew a deep breath and drummed my fingers on the desk. Annoyance tightened my jaw, but then an idea struck me. I couldn't summon Alvin—he'd ensured that by destroying Frank's Sumerian summoning circle—but there *was* a way to reach the underworld. I scanned the list of phone numbers I'd found in the top drawer and quirked a smile. Yes, that might just work.

I picked up Frank's desk phone and dialed the IT Help Desk.

My smile faded when another automated voice answered, speaking in halting tones that sounded as though each word was recorded independently of the others and not part of a cohesive sentence. It was even worse than the extended warranty calls. The voice blandly informed me of service hours and potential wait times and directed me to the Help Desk website for faster service.

Not likely. I hadn't the faintest clue how to use a computer.

After what seemed like a lifetime of irrelevant information, the automated voice asked me to briefly describe my problem.

"I would like to speak to Alvin Bureaucracy."

"I'm sorry, that … isn't an … available … option. Please restate … your problem."

"Connect me to the Department of Bureaucratic Torments."

"I'm sorry, that … isn't an … available … option. Please restate … your problem."

"I'm the Grim Reaper trapped in a human body, and I want to talk to a demon about an ancient Sumerian spell reversal!"

"I'm sorry, that … isn't—"

"I know, you useless machine! Just let me talk to someone who isn't a lumpy scrap of hardware!"

"Okay, so you have a … hardware problem. Connecting you … to one of our … agents. Estimated wait time is"—pause—"ninety-three minutes."

I slumped back and blew out a breath. Tinny music filled my ear. Nothing for it but to wait for whatever tormented soul was assigned to help with hardware problems.

Contrary to popular belief, Hell wasn't all fire, brimstone, and demons dancing around with pitchforks. Not anymore. Most damned souls ended up in the Department of Bureaucratic Torments on Hell's second level, a cubicle farm where souls were condemned to an eternity of customer service. It was a cruel punishment, but a useful one, and Hell had learned that nothing broke a spirit more thoroughly than providing unhelpful service with a smile. Most Earth-based corporations and all the Hell-based ones used their services. Needless to say, all contracted government IT services were based in Torments.

I noted the time on Frank's wall clock and kicked my heels onto the desk. I listened to the tinny music's repeating melody and waited. I slouched lower and rested my head on the back of Frank's chair. This would be a long wait, might as well get comfortable. I closed my eyes and let my mind drift.

A young woman's crisp voice jolted me awake.

"Can I have your computer name and MAC address?"

I sat bolt upright, fumbled and caught the phone, then brought it back to my ear.

"Yes! Hello. Alvin?"

"No, my name's Abigail. You said you have a hardware problem?"

"Not as such. Can you connect me to Alvin Bureaucracy?"

"I'm ... sorry, but this isn't a switchboard. This is a help desk. Do you have a computer problem I can help with?"

"I need to talk to Alvin. It is, quite literally, a matter of life and death."

"If this is an emergency, I recommend hanging up and dialing 911."

"Is that Alvin's direct number?"

"No," she said, frustration seeping into her professional tone. Her voice reminded me of a younger Cora, with the same flat sternness that had preceded all that yelling this morning. "911 is the number for emergency services. You know, to call an ambulance or fire truck?"

This wasn't getting me anywhere.

Wait a second. That voice. "Did you say your name was Abigail? Abigail Knowles?" Was this Cora's deceased daughter?

There was a long silence on the other end before she said, "I never gave my last name. Who are you?" The clacking of a keyboard sounded in the background. "The system registered your name as 'Grim Reaper.' Is this some sort of crank call?"

I drew a deep breath. Should I admit my identity? No. If the wrong demon in Hell heard about my plight, the Auditor would track me down in a heartbeat. But I doubted Abigail would help me unless she believed I knew what I was talking about.

"I know that you are a soul damned to Torments for an eternity of customer service. I know—"

"Watch what you say," Abigail hissed, her voice low and tense. "I don't know who you are, but these calls are monitored. *Nobody* is supposed to know about Torments. They're pretty serious about keeping it a secret, too. Some Hell-spawned nightmare is probably on its way to you already."

"No, they wouldn't send a nightmare. Those were restricted to Hell's sixth level. Can you connect me to the head of the Department of Bureaucratic Torments or not? I wasn't lying about this being a life and death situation."

Abigail sighed. "Normally, I could. But something's going on down here that has *everyone* walking on eggshells. They'd notice. The Auditor himself—oh, shit!"

The line abruptly went dead.

"Hello? Abigail?" I tapped the telephone but only received a dial tone. I clutched the plastic receiver tightly, then slammed it down.

Damn. I'd probably just tipped the Auditor off that something was wrong. If he caught me like this, trapped in a human body, he would happily drag me straight to Hell just so he could take my place. He'd always wanted my job. The Rules governing spiritual matters forbade him from interfering with Death's duties, but I wasn't Death anymore. Just a dying human.

Fear twisted my stomach. I thrust myself to my feet, knocking the office chair back. I needed to leave, now.

The door creaked as I edged it open. I glanced up and down the drab corridor. The path was clear. No demons, and no Sam Davidson with his blessed letter opener.

I slipped out and strode toward the cubicle farm. I paused at the edge of the low-ceilinged room and scanned for trouble. Cora was chatting with a coworker leaning on her cubicle wall. Everyone else was hunched over their desks, unhappy rats working hard without thought toward escaping their maze.

Wait, no. On second glance, they weren't working. They were either playing on their cell phones or eating packed lunches. Sandwiches, salads, and microwaved leftovers mingled with the underlying smell of mildew and despair. None of the auditors paid me the slightest attention.

I strode down the right-hand aisle toward the room's far corner where Lucy sat. She was typing at her computer and seemed to be the only employee doing any real work. She caught my eye as I passed and waved for my attention. Reluctantly, I stopped.

"I got those medical bills from Mrs. Lisle, but she said she has more that aren't scanned in. What a mess! It'll take weeks to sort it all out."

"You don't have weeks," I said. She'd be on her way to Purgatory by Friday then off to either eternal bliss or eternal torment depending on her Judgment. "Have the updated audit ready for review by Thursday."

"Why the rush?" Lucy's brows furrowed. "Is the district director whining about his backlog again?"

"You said it yourself. This audit is late and if it's not done by Thursday, it won't get done. The Lisle family doesn't deserve to have this hanging over them."

"That's a bit harsh. You know I'll finish it; I just need more—"

"Thursday!" I barked, drawing a few eyes. The elevator dinged open, and I glanced up. My heart skipped a beat as a brutish, over-muscled demon strode forth like he owned the place and stopped to survey the room. His tight gray suit's severe cut hinted at segmented Roman armor, merely pretending at civility, while the twin scimitars on his back spoke of how thin that polite veneer truly was. Three parallel scars sliced across his face from his curled left horn to the sharp corner of his right jaw.

Xandu, one of the Auditor's minions. He might look like a mindless brute, but Xandu was a bloodhound at sniffing out discrepancies in the record. And then dispatching said discrepancies with those scimitars on his back. Xandu had been a warrior long before he became a bureaucrat.

An IRS auditor blindly walked through the demon and onto the elevator, and then paused as a shudder ran through him. The demon ignored the intrusion and scanned the room with blood-red eyes.

I averted my gaze so he wouldn't know I'd seen him. So he wouldn't meet my gaze and read my soul. My heart hammered in my chest. "I have to run," I said quietly to

Lucy, "but please do as I ask."

Her lips pursed. "Sounded more like a demand, but you're the boss. I'll get it done."

"Thank you." The Lisle audit didn't really matter, not in the grand scheme, but I liked the thought of doing something useful. Of helping a family in need.

Was that how Frank had felt? Was that why he helped taxpayers get refunds? I shook my head, unable to reconcile the evil mastermind who'd taken my place with the kind of man who would go out of his way to help others.

The demon flowed into motion, marching down the center aisle with military precision, shoulders back, gaze fixed on the hallway that led toward Frank's office.

I stepped away from Lucy's cubicle and headed for the stairs beyond the elevator. I didn't scurry, but tension made every step sound like a drumbeat in my ears. I popped the door open and glanced back just in time to see Xandu disappear into the hallway. He'd be back once he saw that I wasn't in Frank's office.

I scrambled downstairs, crashed through the exit, and sprinted across the parking lot.

Chapter 10

A PROMISE MADE

MY BURST OF SPEED ended at the main road where I stopped to gasp deep lungsful of air. I leaned on a street-lamp. Stars sparkled at the edges of my vision, and I suspected that I'd run more today than Frank's body had run in the past year. Or in his entire lifetime.

Frank's heart gave a warning flutter, and I forced myself upright. After several deep breaths of the crisp mountain air, I started walking down the cracked sidewalk toward Frank's house. I couldn't return to the office. I could have hailed a cab but felt the need to walk and think. To mull over the nature of the evil mastermind behind my predicament. Once Alvin returned with my spell reversal, I would confront Frank Totmann, and I wanted no surprises.

Bright sunlight reflected off glass-sided buildings and the city's constant breeze tugged at my suit, making the brown jacket flap like a tiny cape. The city itself was a strange combination of low-rise buildings and single-story shops interspersed with housing developments. The Land of Evil Auditors was the tallest building for miles around, casting its dark shadow across the parking lot I'd left behind. My stomach growled as I walked, but I ignored it, following the route that Louis the cabbie had driven yesterday.

My thoughts circled like water down a drain. How could I have been so stupid as to call Hell directly? In my impatience to talk to Alvin, I'd alerted the Auditor that something was wrong and put his hound firmly on my trail. And I was no closer to a solution than before I'd called. If anything, I'd made things worse.

I worried about how the call with Abigail had ended. Had I gotten her in trouble as well? Hell's minions were ever inventive in their retributions upon souls who displeased them. Not that I was in any position to help her. I couldn't even help myself.

I reached a wide intersection and stopped to let traffic flow past. While pedestrian fatalities were less frequent than vehicular ones, I'd reaped plenty of souls from crosswalks. I knew better than to charge across. I looked both left and right, waited for a few cars to pass, then headed for the far side.

Screeching tires and a blaring horn nearly gave me a heart attack. A red pickup jacked up on enormous tires rocked to a stop, its grill only inches from my left shoulder. I jumped aside, clutched my chest, and swore.

Where the *hell* had that come from?

The driver honked again.

"All right!" I yelled. "I'm moving!" I stepped past the truck and saw two more cars in the intersection behind it, all turning from the cross street. With an apologetic wave, I rushed across the intersection.

I drew a deep breath once I reached the relative safety of the sidewalk. If I wasn't careful, I wouldn't survive long enough to track Frank down. And dying wasn't how I wanted to meet him again. He would have all the power then, and I wasn't ready to have my soul reaped.

My best solution—my *only* solution—was Alvin and that spell reversal. Where the hell was he?

By the time I reached Frank's house, my feet ached, and my lungs were burning again. Brown grass crunched underfoot as I trod across his yard, too exhausted to bother trudging to the front walk.

Inside, I was again assaulted by the overwhelming stench that was Frank's house. My nose wrinkled, but I flopped onto his couch with a relieved sigh. My feet throbbed. Frank's heart pounded in my chest.

A slight flutter twitched behind my ribs, and then pain pierced my right side. My breath hissed between my teeth. Was this another heart attack?

I drew a half-dozen deep breaths, and the pain in my side eased. No, not a heart attack. I'd just pushed this body too hard. I needed to be more careful. I did *not* want to die. Not only would it be infinitely embarrassing to have a hack like Frank reap my soul, but I was not prepared to face Judgment.

I'd already avoided that fate once.

The flutter behind my ribs increased briefly, as if in counterargument to my desires, then faded away. I drew and released several more breaths and felt my heart rate slow.

I jumped when fifteen pounds of fluffy white Diana

landed in my lap. Piercing green eyes gazed up at me, and the cat gave an inquisitive, "Prrrow?" I ran a finger along her spine.

"Hello, little one. Did you miss me?"

A rumbling purr erupted from her, and she arched her spine against my fingers. I scratched her back and Diana circled my lap, her purr increasing in volume. Her bottlebrush tail slid beneath my nose, making it twitch and leaving long white hairs in my beard. I pushed the tail aside and gave her another pet.

Evelyn had taught me to pay attention to cats. The sneaky little brutes, as she called them, always knew more than they let on. Evelyn had a number of colorful names for cats. Chaos agents, tiny terrors, furry death. Yet, despite Evelyn's vehement claims of distrust, she'd always had a moment to spare for cats. A caress in passing or a murmur in their ear, always delivered with a thoughtful half-smile.

"So, my little chaos agent," I asked Diana as she settled into a loaf on my lap, "tell me about Frank. What kind of man is he?"

She answered by butting her head against my left hand, which had stopped petting her. I resumed my ministrations. Her fur was long and soft. Well groomed.

"He's a man who loves his cat. He cared for you, my tiny terror, better than he did himself or others. Which makes me wonder … did he love Cora? Or was he just using her to get ingredients for his spells?"

Diana began kneading my lap, her purr vibrating my legs. Sharp claws pricked through my pants.

"Ouch." I twitched. Diana dug deeper, alternating paws. "Ouch! That hurts!" I leapt up and Diana tumbled from my lap. She landed on her feet, eyed me reproachfully, then sauntered toward the kitchen. Her tail twitched indignantly.

I scratched at my legs where she'd gouged me, and my stomach rumbled. "Yes, lunch is a good idea. It's hard to concentrate with hunger gnawing my insides." I followed her to the kitchen and turned on the light. My eyebrows rose in surprise at the clean floor that greeted me. The food bag that had spilled yesterday lay empty and shredded in the corner. "You ate all of that?"

In answer, Diana meowed and butted my shin with her head. She purred loudly and rubbed against my legs with all her strength. My stomach gave a sympathetic growl.

"All right, all right. I'll see what I can find."

I opened the refrigerator to see what Frank had left me.

Not much. Beer, soda, an assortment of condiment bottles, and several Styrofoam containers. I opened one and found cold chicken. Perfect.

I tossed a drumstick to Diana and grabbed one for myself. She leapt like the hunter she was and tore into the flesh. My bite was more reserved. It tasted surprisingly good, salty and greasy, though nothing near the quality of last night's Jägerschnitzel. My stomach rumbled, urging haste, and I soon matched Diana's ferocity. After lunch I'd dig deeper into Frank's office. Try to learn more about what made him tick.

Frank's cell phone rang. I dug it out of my pocket and accepted the call with greasy fingers.

"Hello?"

"Hi, I'm calling about your car's extended warranty," that infernal mechanical voice said cheerfully.

"I don't have a car!"

"According to our records, your Honda Accord—"

"Stop calling me!" I jabbed the red END button.

I glared at the phone then dropped it onto the counter and retrieved another chicken leg.

The cursed thing rang again.

Lips pursed, I answered.

"Look, you mechanical misfit, if you don't stop calling about my bloody extended warranty, I will be forced to take extreme measures. I don't know if you have a mechanical soul, but I know demons who would love to tear you apart just to find out."

There was a moment of silence before a woman whispered, "Is this Frank Totmann?"

I almost said no but realized that I still needed to maintain my cover. I sidestepped the question. "How can I help you?"

She chuckled. "Would you believe that I'm calling about your extended warranty?"

"Do you want me to hang up?"

"No," she said, "Sorry. This is Abigail, we spoke earlier?"

My eyebrows climbed up my forehead. I should have recognized her voice. "Your call cut off. What happened?"

"The demon in charge of my cubicle cluster caught me going off-script. I've been demoted from the Customer Service Department to the Customer Annoyance Department. I really am calling you about your extended warranty. Are you interested?"

"No."

"Good. It's a scam."

"You're off-script again. I thought calls were monitored?"

"They are, but my cubicle-mate says that we make so many calls in Customer Annoyance that the administration doesn't bother listening to them all. We're clear, and I have questions."

"As do I." Most importantly, where was Alvin? I so wished the little miscreant hadn't destroyed that Sumerian summoning circle downstairs.

"Mine first. How do you know about Torments?"

So many possible answers to that one. "I have seen it with my own eyes."

"Fantastic. How did you escape?"

That's what she was after? "Escape isn't an option. Souls only traverse the realms in one direction. You live, you die, then you move on to your final destination after Judgment."

"I was never judged. There's been a mistake."

"Sorry, not my department."

"So, what is your department?"

Damn, I walked into that one. Before I could answer, however, Abigail swore.

"Wait, the system registered your name earlier as Grim

Reaper. Sonofabitch! You're him. Black cloak, scythe, shiny skull?"

I sighed. "Yes. I am the Grim Reaper, terror of men's souls. We've met, as you may recall. Just over two years ago."

"You don't sound the same. Your voice boomed like a bass drum before. What happened?"

I sighed again and mumbled under my breath, "You're more intuitive than your mother."

Abigail's voice sharpened. "How do *you* know my mom?"

"We ... went on a date last night—"

"Oh, God."

"—and it turned out quite lovely. She's a charming woman with a vibrant thirst for life."

"Stop. Please stop talking."

"At breakfast this morning she said—"

"You stayed the night! Oh. My. God. My mom is dating the Grim Reaper. She has the worst tastes in men!"

"To be fair, she did not know my identity at the time."

"But she does now? What'd you do, kill her just to prove who you were?"

"No! I don't kill people! I merely reap souls. No, Cora

and I argued this morning and, well, the truth all came out. I'm trapped in Frank Totmann's body, whom she'd *thought* she was dating, and now she wants nothing to do with me."

"Good," Abigail said, quite firmly.

I pursed my lips but left that comment unremarked. "You mentioned that Hell is in an uproar. Explain."

"I need something in return."

"That's not how this works. I answered your question, now you have to answer mine."

"Is that some kind of rule when making a deal with Death?"

"No. It's common courtesy. So, why is Hell in an uproar?"

Abigail paused for a moment before she said, "Everyone's walking around on eggshells. Something about a possible reorganization."

"But they just reorganized four hundred years ago. What's the rush?"

"Rumors say it's something big. A fundamental shift in soul management. The Auditor's involved somehow, but no one will say *what* the big deal is."

A chill danced down my spine. He knew. The Auditor had been angling for my job since the day I got it. He wasn't happy being Hell's final arbiter of the Rules, though he was well-suited for the role. If he managed to take my place, that *would* result in a fundamental change in soul management. And not a change for the better.

Abigail continued talking. "There are rumblings about some new player that has even the Auditor scared."

My eyebrows furrowed. "New player?"

"I haven't heard his name yet, everyone talks about him in whispers, but apparently he wants to expand Hell's influence deeper into the mortal realm."

"New player?" I repeated, trying to wrap my head around the concept. "No, that's not possible. It must be the Auditor flexing his political muscle."

"Or it could be someone new muscling in to make things worse for everyone. Seems like a proper demon thing to do."

"It's a matter of ... biology I suppose you might call it, though that's not entirely accurate. Angels and demons don't reproduce at the same breakneck speed as humans. And thankfully with none of that ghastly body fluid swapping or childbirth. No, new spirits are born from powerful emotional events, both good and evil. Those new spirits are subordinate to their ancient predecessors, like the Auditor and I, who predate Adam and Eve. New spirits have no political power, so this 'new player' can only be an ancient demon. My money is on the Auditor. He's vile, ambitious, and ruthless. And he wants my job."

There was silence on the other end as Abigail considered what I'd said, so I returned to my original request. "I *need* to talk to Alvin Bureaucracy, head of the Department of Bureaucratic Torments."

"I ... may be able to help you. But I really do need something in return."

"I can't bring you back from the dead. That's a one-way street."

She snorted. "I figured that part out. No, I need something simpler. A name."

"Whose?"

"Someone down here who can help me. I'm not supposed to be here, but Hell doesn't exactly have a complaints department."

"You used to work there. Listening to complaints *is* part of the Customer Service Department."

"Ain't that the truth," she said wryly. "But I need to address a problem *internal* to Hell."

I frowned. "Don't expect sympathy from any denizen there. But I know the spirits running Purgatory and can inquire about your case the next time I see them. It might take some time before that happens considering my current predicament, but an inquiry from Death carries weight in Purgatory."

Abigail blew out a long breath and then chuckled bitterly. "I'm sentenced to an eternity in Torments, so I suppose there's no rush. You promise you'll talk to them?"

"I am incapable of lying."

"Really? Huh. In that case, thank you." There was silence again before she said, "Alright, let's see if I can connect you to Alvin. Good luck, and don't forget me."

"I won't." I smiled as the line clicked. Finally, a soul who was willing to help me. She was dead, but who am I to judge?

The phone rang. I willed Alvin to answer, but he did not. After thirty rings, I disconnected with a heavy sigh. I was a fool to put all my trust in Alvin. He had forsaken me. Or forgotten me. It made no difference.

I would have to solve my mortality problem on my own.

Chapter 11

THE COMA CONUNDRUM

MY THOUGHTS SWIRLED AS I retrieved one of Frank's sodas from the fridge and returned to the living room. I dropped onto the couch and threw my feet onto his coffee table, nudging aside a pizza box to make space. The couch was surprisingly comfortable, molded to Frank's shape from the countless hours he must have spent here. I drew a deep breath and the tension in my shoulders eased a little. I opened the soda with a minimum of fumbling and stared blankly at Frank's massive television.

Learning more about Frank's personality felt trivial in light of Alvin's abandonment, leaving me with one burning question.

How the hell was I going to reverse Frank's spell?

Research into ancient magics was not my forte, and I didn't have anyone I could turn to. Cora might have helped me with her skills at occult research, but that door was closed. I pursed my lips and sipped the soda. My tongue curled at the over-sweet orange flavor, but I was thirsty after my walk and the bubbles tingled delightfully on my palate. Like last night's beer, but without the swampy aftertaste.

Perhaps learning more about Frank's personality *was* the answer here. I needed to look at this from a different perspective. How would *Frank* tackle this problem? I eyed the living room. Packed bookcases held nothing of interest—I'd perused them yesterday—but they got me thinking. Books contain information. I just needed the right book. Should I try a library? How would I even find one?

I eyed the black screen before me. No. Books were not the only source of information in today's world. Mankind had invented the internet. I wasn't entirely sure how to access it, but I remembered a soul in Bangkok last month. He'd died with a disturbing array of sordid images and information displayed on his big-screen television. He'd called himself a hacker—whatever that meant—and had been rather desperate to delete something called his 'browser history.'

I had a big-screen television. Let's see what I could do with it.

It took me nearly twenty minutes to turn the infernal thing on. Most of that time was spent trying to find the remote control—I did know a *little* about modern technology—but the elusive plastic wand won its game of hide-and-seek. I then fumbled around the edges of the big screen before finding a button that made it flash to life.

I dropped back onto the couch. A brief banner at the top of the screen named the current program as *Another Day in Paradise*. It was some sort of drama with dark lighting, moody actors, and an overabundance of betrayal and misunderstanding. This wasn't what I needed, but at least the television was *on*. Now to find a browser.

I was digging into the cushions beside me for the remote control when Diana leapt onto my lap. I tried pushing her off, but she wove through my hands in a way that somehow made my dislodgement efforts turn into pets along her spine and neck.

"Do you mind?" I said. "I'm a bit busy."

She didn't mind me at all. After a brief dance around my hands, she settled into a purring lump. I was trapped. Her claws once again dug into my legs in some misguided pleasure ritual, but I slipped my fingertips under her paws to preclude the worst of her happy abuse. With a sigh, I returned my focus to the screen.

Watching *Another Day in Paradise*'s intense drama, I quickly forgot all thoughts of remote controls, misused magic, or research. I knew that the show was fiction but was intrigued in spite of myself.

My fingers massaged Diana's spine as I watched, entranced. I'd always found human emotions unfathomably complex, much like the plotline I was watching, but I suddenly felt as though I'd stumbled upon a source of grand insights into the human psyche.

If I could only understand it.

After nearly an hour, made longer with frustrating advertisement interruptions, I concluded that Felicity, the protagonist, was in her own personal hell, trapped without comfort or hope. Not that she was an innocent, but it appeared that the mistakes of her past were being revisited upon her ten-fold. There was no sense of justice through it all. Merely vengeance, judgment, and pain.

My thoughts returned to Abigail. Despite being trapped in Torments, Cora's daughter seemed to be a caring soul. She'd tried to help me, and what hope had I given her in return? A vague promise. But what else did I have to offer?

I kneaded around Diana's collar, making her bell jingle lightly before my fingers froze. Cats could travel between realms at will. Diana was incredibly self-centered, as were all cats and most humans I'd met, but perhaps I could convince her to help.

I lowered my face until my lips were just above the sleepy cat's ears. "Diana, I need your help."

Her purrs continued unabated.

I wrapped my hands under her chest and lifted the cat until we were eye-to-eye. She blinked sleepily but her green-eyed gaze met mine.

"I need you to travel to the underworld. I have a ... a friend there who needs comfort." It felt odd to call anyone a friend, but I could think of no better term for Abigail, despite our brief acquaintance.

Diana struggled in my grasp, and I set her on the floor.

Her tail twitched in irritation, and she eyed me like a goddess contemplating vengeance. Cats and crows were often used by spirits as messengers between realms, though cats were dreadfully unreliable. I didn't know if I had the power to command her in this human form. I leaned down.

"Find Abigail Knowles. She's in Torments, in the Department of Customer Annoyance."

Diana blinked but didn't move.

"Please, she needs you. I will find you more chicken when you return. Would you like more chicken?"

Diana licked her chops, but I couldn't tell if she understood me. With another twitch of her tail, the cat stalked to a small cardboard box in the corner by a bookshelf and leapt inside. She settled down until only the tufts of her white ears were visible. I sighed. No, she hadn't understood me.

An abrupt change on the screen drew my attention. *Another Day in Paradise* had ended while I talked to Diana, replaced by a newscast.

Ah, much better!

A perky middle-aged woman with puffy platinum-blonde hair and a wide smile appeared on the screen. Once she introduced herself, her expression turned to one of overwhelming concern. "Next on the Midday News, 'The Coma Conundrum: Epidemic or Miracle?'" The screen changed to a middle-aged Hispanic nurse standing in front of an emergency room admittance desk. Her eyes were tired but intense, and her long black hair wisped out of her tight bun. The banner at the bottom of the screen identified her as Candice Lisle, Wehling Memorial ER Nurse.

The name tickled the back of my brain before I snapped my fingers. Ah, the audit that Lucy was working on. Candice Lisle looked as fierce as her name suggested. The Kandake of Meroe, mistranslated as 'Candice' by the Greeks, were once Ethiopian queens of great renown. Every Candice I met carried a bit of that name's ancient fire in their soul, and Nurse Lisle was no exception.

Her lips pursed as the male reporter with an aggressive tone asked, "What's Wehling Memorial doing about the spike in coma cases?"

"First, we're not the only hospital who reported this. And second, you say 'spike in coma cases' like it's a problem."

"Isn't it?"

"The rise of coma cases corresponds to a matching decline of mortality rates. Simply put, people aren't dying and *that's* a good thing. Here in the ER, we're seeing folks survive injuries that should have killed them."

"So, you believe this is a miracle?"

Nurse Lisle shrugged. "God works in mysterious ways. I'm just glad these patients have more time."

I huffed at the screen. God had nothing to do with this. I doubted he even cared. No, their survival was a mistake by an interloping Reaper who didn't know what he was doing. And survival wasn't a good thing. If humanity had already noticed Frank's failures to reap the dead, then I'd bet my last breath that *Hell* had noticed.

The screen shifted again to a handsome man in an expensive black suit with silver hair styled in the well-combed fashion of politicians everywhere. He stood behind a podium at a press conference. The man looked familiar, but all politicians look the same to me. Monied and arrogant, but with a brilliant smile that flashed white against medium-brown skin which could have originated anywhere from India to Brazil.

Damien Nigel, the banner said. Independent Presidential Candidate. Instinctively I knew that wasn't his real name. I couldn't read his soul through the television screen, but this was a man with secrets.

I snorted. Of course he had secrets. He was a politician. They lie worse than demons. He flashed a sparkling smile at the camera.

"It's wonderful to hear that folks are surviving such terrible accidents and injuries, but I worry about hospital capacity. If I'm elected, I'll ensure increased funding to medical facilities across the nation. The United States will lead the way as the world deals with this unprecedented Coma Conundrum."

Hmmm, I hadn't considered the problem of hospital capacity. Perhaps this guy did have a head on his shoulders. He was at least thinking about the big picture.

"I'll be in Colorado Springs this evening on my campaign tour, and I intend to visit Wehling Memorial Hospital to see this phenomenon for myself."

Someone off-screen, a woman's voice this time, said, "Many have attributed these survivals to divine intervention. What are your thoughts, Mr. Nigel?"

Disgust and rage flickered across that dashing face so fast that I might have imagined it. He flashed his politician's smile and—

Recognition slammed into me. That tickling concern

that I knew this man's face became a dead certainty. "No. He can't be," I said under my breath.

Nigel ... the *Demigod*?

I'd never met him up close, but I knew that face. Damien Nigel had the same broad shoulders, defiant arrogance, and perfectly charming smile as the last time I'd seen him.

On the last day I'd seen Evelyn; before he dragged her into Abaddon.

I shook my head, swearing softly. No, this couldn't be *that* Nigel. It was impossible. *Nobody* escaped Abaddon. True, Frank now held Abaddon's key, but even if he accidentally opened Hell's seventh level, Damien Nigel had clearly been around longer than two days. This politician was just a doppelganger.

He had to be.

I'd missed Nigel's response, and the screen returned to the puffy-haired news anchor. "There you have it," she crooned. "With Nigel on the job, we have nothing to worry about! Now we turn to the ongoing drama at the Cheer and Dance Nationals." The screen flicked to what looked like a massive brawl inside a high school gymnasium.

I stopped listening and pulled myself out of Frank's decadently comfortable couch. A Demigod's doppelganger wasn't my concern.

Miraculous survivals were. This Damien Nigel had the right idea. I needed to see this Coma Conundrum for myself.

"Diana," I addressed the cardboard box, which ignored me. "I'm heading out. While I'm gone ... are you paying attention?" I stepped over and glanced down into the box. It was empty.

"Diana?" I called.

Silence answered. I shrugged and retrieved Frank's phone and Louis's card. I'd need a ride to Wehling Memorial Hospital.

It was time to visit some lingering souls.

Chapter 12

A QUESTION OF TIME

By the time Louis honked from the curb, the sun had disappeared behind the ridgeline, leaving behind lingering twilight. I'd swapped Frank's suit jacket for a puffy black coat and stepped out into the incessant wind. The jacket flared around me, so I held it close to my body and trudged to the cab.

The familiar undercurrent of vomit overlaid by artificial lemon assaulted me when I opened the cab's door, but I refrained from comment. I did, however, congratulate myself on how many doors I'd navigated today without fumbling. I really *was* getting the hang of this human thing.

"The Fred Wehling Memorial Hospital, Louis." Knowing what to expect from Louis's driving, I braced myself against the door and seat and added, "No rush," hoping to forestall the worst of his driving.

I don't know why I bothered.

"No problem, Grim!" Louis flipped a U-turn and sped out of Frank's neighborhood. He blew through the stop sign at the corner, and his gaze flicked to the mirror. "You don't look so good, brother, and we're headed to the hospital. Everything alright?"

"I ... don't like driving. It's one of mankind's deadliest habits. Trust me, I would know."

He nodded. "That's an interesting insight coming from a coroner. I got seatbelts back there if you want 'em."

Yeah, right. Like I would tie myself to this death trap. We reached a red light and Louis slammed on the brakes. I rocked forward and almost hit my face on the seatback in front of me. Clearly my 'interesting insights' weren't enough to curb Louis's driving habits.

Perhaps a seatbelt wasn't such a horrible idea.

I found it behind my right shoulder and pulled the belt across my lap and chest. It took a few tries to figure out where to attach the little metal plate, but finally it clicked into the seat by my left hip.

Good timing, too. The light turned green, and Louis sped through the intersection, weaving around the car ahead of him. He glanced back again. "Well, I did it. Apologized to Nicole for buying her a vacuum on our anniversary."

"And how did that turn out?"

Louis waggled a hand as he braked for the next traffic light. "I'm not on the couch anymore, but she's still pissed. I need some major brownie points but don't know what to buy. Everyone I ask says to buy flowers, but do you know how expensive roses are? I just blew all my money on that stupid vacuum!"

I scratched my jaw and considered. I've never understood why presenting cut flowers on the verge of death was a symbol of love. Shouldn't you present a freshly planted seed or a potted plant instead? Something that could grow and be nurtured into beautiful and thriving life? Humans are odd.

As Louis turned onto the freeway onramp, I said, "I'm no expert on romance. What made Nicole fall for you in the first place?"

Louis's lips pursed, and he scratched the back of his neck. I wished he'd keep his hands on the wheel. A horn blared from behind us as he violently—and one-handed-ly—changed lanes.

"We met in high school but didn't start dating until senior year," he said. "Man, we were inseparable! Did everything together."

"And do you still? Do everything together, I mean." I flinched and sucked air between my teeth when Louis cut to the right between two semi-trucks. He didn't even notice my reaction and hit an offramp at speed.

"Not really," he said. "Life kinda got in the way over the last few years. We've been fighting more too. I mean, we always fought, but I figured that was just so we could make up ... if you know what I mean." He waggled his eyebrows at me in the mirror. I did not know what he meant. "But recently it's just been fighting without making up. We both work long hours, and all our free time is taken with the boys, sports, bills, and, you know, life."

"Then perhaps that is the answer you seek. Don't give Nicole expensive flowers that will die within a week. Give her something more precious. Give her your time." I thought about Louis's soul and the death I'd read in it.

Seven years wasn't very long. "Life is fleeting, Louis. Spend the time you have with the ones you love before it's too late."

Downtown traffic forced Louis to slow. He looked thoughtful for a moment before glancing in the mirror again. "You lost someone, didn't you?"

I nodded but said nothing, that damned ancient battle-field flashing through my mind. The blood and sand. The sound of Evelyn's scream that abruptly cut off. I shuddered and forced my fists to unclench.

Louis glanced into the mirror. Perhaps it was something in my expression that stopped him, but for once he didn't ask more probing questions. We rode in silence for a couple of blocks before he turned into the Wehling Memorial parking lot.

I paid him, fought with the seatbelt until it finally released, and stepped from the cab. Before I closed the door, Louis leaned over the seat and caught my gaze.

"You really think my time is what Nicole wants?"

"I wouldn't presume to know what she wants. But I suspect it is what she needs. Time is the one commodity everyone squanders; yet they always complain about never having enough time when they die."

Louis quirked a smile. "Ain't that the truth! Ya know, you should write a book. A Coroner's Advice for Life!"

A half-smile pulled at my lips. "Thank you, but I have other priorities at the moment." I waved toward Wehling Memorial, which loomed like a titan behind me.

Louis gave a thumbs up, I closed the door, and he tore out of the lot, tires squealing.

I glanced around, saw a sign that said EMERGENCY, and followed the arrow down the sidewalk. Nurse Lisle worked in the emergency room, so I hoped she could help me find the souls Frank had failed to reap. The ones suffering from this Coma Conundrum.

The whole matter bothered me. Humanity only got so much time on this mortal coil, no matter how much they begged. Well, these poor souls were finally getting their extra time, but I doubted they were enjoying it.

I lengthened my stride. Time to see just how bad Frank's screw-ups really were.

Chapter 13

A State of Undeath

Wehling Memorial Hospital was a massive, sprawling facility with rust-red bricks and mirrored windows. Despite looking like its architect had randomly stacked circular children's blocks together and called it a day, the hospital managed to appear sleek and modern. It took several minutes to navigate a warren of sidewalks outside the building to a circle drive with a covered entrance that said Emergency Trauma Center in bold red letters. A handful of ambulances and police cars sat in the drive.

I eyed the double-wide glass doors as I approached. No

handles, knobs, or levers. Great. How on earth was I supposed to open—

The doors slid apart of their own accord, revealing a short entryway with matching double doors at the other end. I smiled and strode through. What a pleasant surprise. *Every* door should be automatic.

The second set of doors slid open, and I was assaulted by what sounded like a barroom brawl and the overwhelming odor of sweat and antiseptic. There was an empty reception desk to my left and absolute pandemonium to my right.

The packed waiting room was split into two groups of enraged cheerleaders separated by a thin line of burly officers and burlier nurses. The girls on one side glittered in sequined green leotards with short skirts. The other side looked identical, but in brilliant blue. Bandages, bruises, and slings had been handed out wholesale. The raucous focus of the room was on two blonde girls from opposite sides being forcibly separated by policemen. The cheerleader in green had deep scratches across her face. Her opponent in blue had a hand wrapped in a blood-stained towel.

The officers managed separation. Barely. Volume in the

room lulled a touch before the girl in blue spat, "Bitch."

The girl in green lunged free like a cat trying to escape a bathtub. Over the officer's shoulder she scrambled, claws extended. Both hands latched onto her enemy's hair, and the girls collapsed to the floor in a screeching tangle.

Hmmm. This must be the 'ongoing drama at the Cheer and Dance Nationals' that the news had referenced. The screams sounded like they came from enraged badgers rather than teenage girls.

"Hey!" A woman's sharp voice cut through the noise followed by the resounding *boom* of a door that slammed like impacting artillery. A momentary silence fell over the spandex-clad combatants. Nurse Lisle flew past me from behind the reception desk and sliced through the crowd. The Hispanic woman was shorter than most of the lithe teens, but she exuded an air of competence and control that made girls back away from her.

She pointed a finger at the two on the ground who'd paused mid-scrap. "Try to kill each other on your own time, not mine! You"—she pointed at the one in blue with the bandaged hand—"come with me. You"—she pointed to the other—"sit down until I can free up a room." She then pointed at the largest of the nurses, a hulking woman with a Pacific Islander's complexion, neck tattoos, and twice the muscle of the male officer beside her. "Mary, I need you in charge, not breaking up brawls. That's their job!" Nurse Lisle jabbed a finger at the diminutive officer beside Mary. "I want triage happening before I get back. These girls should be in examination by now!"

Nurse Lisle spun on her heel, gestured imperiously at the cheerleader with the bandaged hand, then led her toward the swinging doors at the back of the waiting area.

There was a moment of stunned silence before Nurse Mary started bellowing orders which, surprisingly, the girls followed.

I abruptly realized that I'd been standing by the entrance entirely too long, slack-jawed and watching like a spectator at a boxing match. I had a coma ward to find.

I followed Nurse Lisle from a discreet distance. I'd hoped to question her about the coma cases, but she wasn't exactly available for a quiet chat. I'd have to find the coma ward myself.

She passed through the swinging doors, which whipped back toward me with a vengeance. I caught them before they slapped me in the face, and I grinned. Yes, I'd figured out this whole door thing. I would not be thwarted! I pushed through. Nurse Lisle was leading her patient down a wide hallway to the right. I turned left.

A rushed bustle of nurses and doctors filled the hall. Tense voices, beeping medical monitors, and the slap of worn sneakers on linoleum created a cacophony of barely controlled chaos. It was a comforting sound. Something I'd come to expect in emergency rooms in big cities.

I glanced at each door as I passed, looking for the coma ward. Death spends a lot of time in hospitals, though I'm not usually constrained to wandering through hallways. I finally asked directions from a young man in a lab coat. He pointed me toward a bank of four elevators in a quiet side hallway. The coma ward overflow was on the third floor. I thanked him and strolled to the elevator bank.

The doors did not open for me.

I frowned. The elevators at the Land of Evil Auditors had always been open before I entered. I looked up, down, left, and right, but saw no handles, knobs, or levers. I pushed on the nearest heavy metal door.

Nothing.

I pressed my hands to it and tried sliding it to the left.

The door didn't slide.

I pushed to the right.

Same lack of result.

I pushed *really hard* to the left.

Stupid, infernal…

I tried *all* the elevators.

Nothing but sweat under my arms and an insistent itch in my beard. I slapped the doors in frustration and stepped back to scratch furiously at my jaw. My steely glare, annoyingly, didn't convince *any* of the stupid elevator doors to open.

Wait, the hospital entry doors had opened automatically when I approached. Perhaps these doors just hadn't seen me.

I returned to the main hall, then sauntered back with deceptive calm. I even whistled.

Nothing.

I repeated the motion but dashed into the side hall.

Still nothing.

My jaw clenched, and I jumped up and down waving my arms so it would see me. "Open, you infernal contraption!"

A hunched older gentleman with a wooden cane and a ring of curly white hair entered the little hallway. He caught me mid-jump. We both paused, eying each other. I straightened, feeling like a fool, and he stepped up beside me. I didn't want to meet his gaze, so I stared at the bloody doors.

They *still* didn't open.

We stood in awkward silence for a moment before the old man leaned forward and pressed a small button between elevators. A button with a little arrow pointing up.

The doors in front of me slid open with a cheerful ding.

Seriously? Now doors have *buttons?* What'll they come up with next? A door you have to *lick* to pass through?

I drew a deep breath and followed the man onto the elevator. He glanced my way. "Which floor?" His voice was thin and timorous.

"Um, the third," I said. He pressed two buttons in a bank of buttons with a shaky hand, and the numbers three and four lit up. "Thank you," I said heartily, and he nodded.

The third floor was much quieter than the ground floor. Following the young man's directions, I wandered a warren of hallways until I found a door with a hastily scrawled sign that read COMA WARD OVERFLOW. In the twenty-four hours since I'd become human, Wehling Memorial already had an overflow problem from the Coma Conundrum. It was a story that I suspected was being replayed in hospitals around the world. I had to reverse Frank's damned spell before things spiraled out of control.

I turned the door lever and pushed.

The door stayed firmly shut. My shoulder rebounded off it as I leaned forward, expecting it to open.

I stepped back, lips pursed, and rubbed my shoulder. Still a touch rattled from my experience with the elevator, I looked around for a button. To the right of the door was a small keypad with a tiny red light above it.

It had ten buttons.

What sadistic madness was this?

I pressed number one.

The light blinked, but nothing happened.

I pressed number two.

Same result. This was as bad the elevators!

When I reached number six, the light blinked rapidly three times and the keypad beeped at me. I tried the door, but it was still locked.

The rumble of small wheels on linoleum drew my attention down the hall to my left. A thin young man with a scruffy beard and shaggy black hair pushed a cleaning cart out of a room three doors down. He wore large black headphones, head bopping in time with whatever he was listening to.

He glanced my way, and I raised an inquiring finger. I was done looking like a fool for the sake of recalcitrant doors. I needed help. The young man dropped his headphones around his neck and ran assessing eyes over me.

"Visitor?" he asked.

"Yes. Can you help me?" I waved toward the keypad.

He rolled his eyes and strode forward, leaving his cart. "Clara downstairs forget to give you a temp badge too? You're my third badge-in today!"

I had no idea who Clara was, but I just raised my hands sheepishly and shrugged. He slid between me and the door and rapidly tapped six numbers into the keypad. The red light turned green, and the door made a loud *click*.

"Thank you," I said. He just gave me a nod and slid his headphones back on before bopping back to his cleaning cart.

A six-digit code? I never would have figured that out. At least I didn't have to lick the door to pass through.

I strode inside. Two rows of partitioned beds greeted me along with the sickly-sweet smell of death, only faintly overlaid with the smell of fresh flowers. Now *that* was a good use for cut flowers. Presented to the dying as a symbol of things to come. Plus, flowers masked the unpleasant odors associated with death.

Indistinct voices sounded from the back right corner, but I couldn't see anybody through the free-standing curtains separating the beds. I moved to the nearest bed on the left side of the room. An elderly woman lay in perfect repose, arms at her sides under a bleached blanket, thin white hair matted to her head with sweat. She had a sunken look to her that made her cheekbones stand out like the rugged Colorado mountains. I peeled back one eyelid and read her soul.

My jaw clenched. She should have died nine hours ago. This poor woman's body had failed, but her soul was fully aware of what was happening in her state of undeath. I'd seen this before; on the one occasion when I'd been restrained from properly reaping souls at their moment of death.

I crossed the aisle to the next patient but pulled up short at the heavyset woman with gray hair sitting in the chair beside the bed. She held the hand of the equally heavy man filling the bed and glanced up as I entered. She eyed my brown tweed pants and puffy black jacket.

"Are you a doctor?"

"No, I'm just visiting." I gestured to the patient. Her husband, I assumed from their matching wedding bands. "How long has he been like this?"

"Since last night. Tommy…" Tears choked her, and she wiped at her eyes. "Tommy came in with severe heartburn then … he just collapsed. They said it was a heart attack, a big one that should have killed him, but he dropped into a coma. Now he won't wake up. Why won't he wake up?" Sad eyes begged me for an answer, even if it was a lie.

I couldn't lie, but I doubted the truth would have helped. Tommy was dead. His body just hadn't realized it yet because his soul was still attached. "I wish that I could help," I said, meaning every word. "Excuse me." I backed into the aisleway.

Is this what would have happened if Sam had stabbed me with his blessed letter opener? He hadn't attacked with intent to kill—he'd hoped that Frank would resume residence—but I wondered if his blessed blade would have severed my soul's connection to Frank's body. Would I have become a ghost? Or would I have ended up like Tommy? It was a chilling thought.

The voices at the back of the room became more distinct, and I glanced up to see Damien Nigel and a white male doctor who looked like he'd attended the same charm school and barber as the politician. Nigel was a large man, fit and muscled, who stood head and shoulders taller than the doctor. A bevy of reporters and aides followed them, though I'm not sure how they'd all fit into that little curtained area with the patient.

The doctor handed Nigel a printout as they strode toward me. "See this flat line here, right before everything starts up again? They all have this, though some more frequently than others. It's like they keep dying, but their souls aren't ready to leave. So, the body just keeps on ticking."

Nigel shook his head. "That isn't right. I'll see what I can do." I stepped back to let them pass, and the doctor cocked a polite eyebrow at Nigel.

"Not questioning your desire to help, Mr. Nigel, but I'm not sure what you *can* do."

"I have ... resources." He glanced toward the aides, and I followed his gaze. My breath caught. One of those aides wasn't human.

He was a demon.

Of average build with plain features and the first

well-pressed suit I'd seen on a demon in centuries, the only indications that this creature wasn't human were his blood-red eyes and the short nubs of horns that poked through his well-coifed hair. I doubted the humans could see him, or they wouldn't have been nearly so calm.

And then it clicked. The truth I'd refused to acknowledge earlier.

Damien Nigel, politician, and Nigel, King of the Demigods were one and the same. It was impossible—I'd sealed Abaddon myself!—but the truth was striding past me in an expensive three-piece suit. My jaw wanted to drop, but I couldn't draw attention to myself. I froze beside the undead woman's bed, watching them pass.

The demon nodded at Nigel and said with a voice smooth as silk, "The Auditor has contingency plans for when Death fails at his assigned duties."

What? What plans? What hell had Frank unleashed by swapping our souls?

The doctor pushed through the door, and the small crowd departed. The door swung shut right in front of the demon-aide, but he just passed through it like the spirit he was.

I drew a shuddering breath. Nigel the Demigod was

back. It was a hard truth to accept. Not that I could do anything about it. Not as a mortal.

I gave them a full minute to clear the hallway before following. Back at the elevators, I pressed the down button and then thrust my hands into the puffy jacket's pockets.

The doors didn't immediately open. As I waited, my thoughts returned to Nigel and his demon aide.

If what he'd said was true, then the Auditor and the Office of Micromanagement would be after me soon.

If they weren't already.

The elevator dinged open, and I stepped inside. As I turned, Frank's cell phone rang.

Despite my failures to reach Alvin, hope once again made my heart leap into my throat at the cheerful jangle.

"Hello? Alvin?"

"Hi, I've been trying to reach you about your car's extended warranty."

"Oh, come on!"

"Our records indicate—"

"No!" I jabbed my finger on the red END button. Jaw clenched, I slammed my fist against the elevator button for the ground floor.

A flash of black cowl slid past the elevator.

"Frank!" I yelled, frozen in surprise.

The overweight buffoon was waltzing down the hall, swinging my scythe like a schoolboy swinging a stick at weeds, without a care in the world. He glanced up at my yell, and froze, eyes widening. He grinned when he recognized me and waved.

"Hiya! How's it goin'?"

The elevator started to close. I lunged forward, wedging myself between the doors. They hit me and pressed briefly. I grunted before they reopened. The delay wasn't much, but it stopped my forward momentum and I stumbled, dropping to one knee. With a curse, I forced myself upright.

I was too slow. Frank threw me a cocky salute, placed both hands on *Grace,* and twisted the scythe's handle.

He disappeared in the space between heartbeats.

"Damn!" I stumbled to a stop. He'd been right there! And I'd lost him. Again. I muttered another curse before stomping back to the elevator. Now what?

The silent hallway offered no answers.

Chapter 14

THE INTERN AND HER SHADOW

WEDNESDAY. HUMP DAY AS humans like to call it. The mid-point of their work week and a time to look forward to the weekend.

I had nothing to look forward to beyond death and damnation.

These cheerful thoughts woke me along with a painful ringing noise. I blinked blearily at the ceiling of Frank's bedroom as the fog of sleep passed. I willed the ringing to stop.

It didn't. I clambered out of bed and stumbled around Frank's bedroom before I pinpointed the source. Frank's cell phone rang cheerily from his jacket, which I'd hung on a hook behind the door. I answered it.

"Hello?"

"Frank! Where the hell are you?" It was Lucy. She hissed the words, as though trying not to be overheard.

"I just woke up," I said and ran a hand through Frank's thinning hair. "I had a late night."

"Seriously? You ditched early yesterday, and now you're partying on a *Tuesday night*? Is this a mid-life crisis?"

More like an end-of-life crisis. "I was at Wehling Memorial Hospital."

There was a sharp intake of breath.

"Not for me," I said. "I was … visiting."

Lucy's relief sounded loud in my ear. "Thank God. Well, hustle your bustle into the office. Your intern has arrived."

My brows drew together. "Intern? I didn't order an intern."

"Well, she's here and looking quite lost. Cora took pity on the poor girl, so you should be okay for a few minutes. But don't take too long. Your sweetheart is saying some surprisingly nasty things about you. Did you two have a fight?"

My jaw clenched. Would Cora tell this intern the truth about me?

I had no idea.

"I'm on my way," I said and disconnected before dialing Louis's number. If anyone could get me to work fast, it was him.

The phone rang five times before going to voicemail. Louis cheerfully declared that he was off shift and probably sleeping, and he provided the number to his dispatch office. I frowned, hung up, and dialed the number he'd given.

A brusque man took my information and offered to send a cab in thirty minutes. I begged that they come sooner but was firmly rebuffed. Resigned, I ordered the cab.

The phone buzzed as he hung up, giving three insistent beeps. I glanced at the screen. It briefly blinked an empty battery image before going dark.

Dead. Great.

I drew a deep breath, then frowned. Something smelled rank, like moldering leaves, but more vibrant and rancid. I sniffed the air more delicately then lowered my nose to my armpit. I jerked back, nose wrinkled. It was me. *I* smelled vibrant and rancid. I glanced at the bedside clock. Could I bathe in thirty minutes?

More importantly, could I survive bathing?

I'd never bathed before—body odor isn't a problem in the spirit realm—but I understood the dangers of the process. Slippery porcelain, unforgiving tile, electric shock. Drowning. The number of souls I reaped from showers and bathtubs was truly appalling.

Yet, such are the perils of mortality. I drew a deep breath and the clock ticked over. Twenty-nine minutes. I sighed.

Like a convict resigned to the gallows, I marched for Frank's bathroom.

***

To my eternal joy, I survived my shower. It was even mildly enjoyable. My beard no longer itched and looked decidedly puffy. My skin tingled with the faint scent of crushed mint and rosemary. Frank's shampoo bottle claimed this was the scent of a phoenix, but I wasn't entirely convinced. Phoenixes smell more like dry ash and blood. Regardless,

I appreciated the evoked image. Like the phoenix, I would rise from the ashes of my defeat and reclaim my position and title. I would be Death once again.

That enthusiasm carried me through my silent cab ride to the office. Unlike Louis, this cabbie seemed incapable of conversation beyond 'where to' and 'that'll be twelve bucks' and he drove like a snail caught napping. Regardless, I entered the Land of Evil Auditors in a cheerful mood.

I stepped from the elevator onto the third floor. Lucy saw me, glanced pointedly at her watch, then cocked an eyebrow at me.

Okay, so I took forty minutes to get here. At least I'd had time to charge Frank's cell phone a little with the cord I'd found by his nightstand. Never mind the time I'd wasted searching for the cord and then figuring out how to plug it in.

Lucy motioned back toward the elevator. "Cora took the intern to IT."

"Got it," I said and spun on my heel to catch the elevator door before it closed. I pressed the button for the basement.

My cheer faded as I descended. The basement. Where

Sam Davidson had attacked me with his blessed blade. Had that been only yesterday?

A niggle of worry crept under my cheer, but I told myself that I'd remain vigilant. No surprises today. The demon hunter wouldn't stab me while people were around, surely. I'd just have to ensure I stayed near other people. I nodded to myself. As far as plans went, it had the value of simplicity.

The elevator door dinged open, revealing the basement's long hallway.

It's long *empty* hallway. Not a soul in sight. Just full supply cages, stained linoleum, and a light at the end of the hall that flickered fitfully.

So much for my simple plan. Silence stretched as the underlying stench of mildew and despair filled the elevator.

Well, there was nothing for it. Once more into the breach, as they say. I set my jaw and strode forth, shoes squeaking and clicking on the linoleum. I tried slowing my pace and adjusting how I stepped, but Frank's shoes insisted on betraying my presence. How do cats walk so quietly? Diana could have snuck through this hallway like a white-furred bandit!

I kept a watchful eye on the Logistics Department's

door as I approached IT. Was Sam inside, waiting to pounce? I grasped IT's door handle, gaze still locked on Sam's door.

A throaty laugh from inside IT made me jump. Cora. I scowled, annoyed at my fears. Sam wasn't the boogeyman waiting to jump out at me. He was just a human.

I twisted IT's door handle and pushed inside.

Cora stood at a high counter with a young woman, whom I assumed was the intern. She had dark skin with matching brown eyes, a broad smile, and curly black hair that framed her face like a halo. A young man with glasses and an enraptured expression listened from behind the counter as the intern told a story, a laptop forgotten between them.

"—but all the little guy *really* wanted was for someone to love him." Her empty hands were cupped as if she were holding something soft and furry.

The young man's enraptured smile went lopsided. "But how did you *know* that?"

She shrugged. "It's a gift."

The door clicked shut behind me, and everybody turned.

Cora's expression cooled, and she crossed her arms.

"Frank. Nice of you to show up."

My jaw clenched. I didn't owe her an explanation. "I understand this young lady is my new intern?"

Cora nodded. "I'd like you to meet Elizabeth Kolnik. Liz, this is ... Frank."

The girl's ready smile faltered at Cora's cold tone, but she stepped forward with an outstretched hand. "Happy to meet you."

I shook her firm grip and gazed into her soul. Elizabeth Kolnik, twenty-three years old, death in ... hmmm, a variable date of death. My eyebrows rose. Variable dates weren't common, but I saw them more often in young people. Free will always trumps fate, so Elizabeth had some monumental choice yet to make in her life.

I also felt something odd as she gripped my hand. Like a tingle in my soul. I felt her emotions and knew that she felt mine. Could she read my soul? Her eyebrows rose in matching surprise, and she released my hand. The tingle stopped.

"You're—" She stopped and obviously changed what she'd intended to say. "Your guest lecture in my Accounting Ethics class was incredible." I suppressed a grimace. Great. She'd met Frank before.

But what had she felt in our brief ephemeral connection? "Well," I said, "if you enjoyed accounting ethics, what made you decide to come *here?* To the Land of Evil Auditors?"

Elizabeth laughed a bright full laugh. "The Land of Evil Auditors. That's good! Nobody likes auditors"—I couldn't agree more—"but the IRS is the only place hiring accountants without experience these days. I hope to turn this internship into a paying job."

Cora eyed me. "I was just telling Elizabeth that she should intern with me. I know you're terribly busy these days ... Frank."

Yes, yes. I know I'm not Frank. She didn't need to keep reminding me that I'd spilled the beans yesterday. Cora stood protectively close to the girl, hovering like a mother hen. Elizabeth was about the same age that Cora's daughter Abigail would have been, had she survived. From the way Cora fingered Abigail's Celtic cross amid her necklaces, I suspected she'd made that connection as well.

Motion to my left caught my eye. I glanced over and lurched back in surprise.

An angel stood in the corner, arms crossed, hidden among the shadows of a metal wall cabinet and a fake palm tree. She was the essence of darkness. Straight black hair, form-fitting black leathers, curved sword at her hip. Her wings and skin were the shade of darkest night, blending with the shadows.

My mouth went dry. She was an impossibility. A ghost. The other half of my heart whom I'd doomed to an eternity of torment over five thousand years ago.

"Evelyn," I whispered. "How...?"

Her chestnut eyes caught my gaze. Shock flashed across her face, quickly replaced by fury. She'd recognized my soul, even if she didn't know this body.

"Grim." Evelyn's voice was rough, as though damaged from too much screaming. She stepped forward and took up position behind Elizabeth's right shoulder like a winged shadow. One wing arched protectively around the girl, and a hand fell to her sword's hilt. She gripped it so tightly her knuckles turned white. "Leave Liz alone."

My mind struggled to comprehend the reality of Evelyn standing before me. Of course, if Nigel was free, why wouldn't Evelyn be free? Yet the sight of her sent my thoughts spiraling, reeling, and I latched onto what was possibly the least important fact of this unfolding tableau.

Evelyn was Elizabeth's guardian angel. Evelyn ... the

former captain of the Heavenly Host answerable only to Gabriel and the Almighty himself. Few humans warranted a guardian angel, let alone one so high up the ranks.

Who *was* this girl?

Cora was eyeing me oddly, her face a mix of worry and unease. No one else in the room, of course, could see Evelyn.

I abruptly realized that I'd spoken Evelyn's name aloud and was staring over Elizabeth's shoulder like a goggle-eyed fool. Damn.

"Frank?" Cora said. "You look like someone just walked over your grave."

I shook myself. "It wasn't *my* grave."

Fire flashed in Evelyn's eyes.

"It didn't have to be mine, either," she growled. "You trapped me in Abaddon, you heartless bastard! All you had to do was wait five more minutes—*five minutes*—and I would have been free. Your impatience cost me five millennia!" Her sword whipped from its sheath. It's tip hovered inches from my nose.

I went very, very still, not even daring to breathe. I knew that blade. Blacker than the Devil's soul and curved like a katana, *Mercy* was the only blade capable of unmaking an immortal soul. Of granting a true death.

And Evelyn looked ready to use it on me.

Cold rage poured from Evelyn, and I took an involuntary step back toward the door. Some of that anger overflowed into Elizabeth, and the girl's brows pinched downward in confusion.

I turned to Cora. "You were right. I ... I don't believe I should take on an intern at this time."

Before anybody could respond, I spun on my heel and fled.

Chapter 15

Out of the Frying Pan

Out of the frying pan and into the fire, so the saying goes. I made it as far as the stairwell before literally running into Sam Davidson. He didn't see me over his armload of small narrow boxes, and I wasn't paying attention as I dashed through the stairwell door.

We collided like twin freight trains. I fell back into the stairwell door, and Sam landed on the cement stairs. His boxes tumbled and bounced between us, several spilling their contents. Toner cartridges, according to the box labels.

"Watch where you're..." Sam said, then stopped, eyes

narrowing in recognition. "Demon."

I'd landed awkwardly on my left hip and held up my right hand, palm out as I tried to get my feet under me. "I don't want trouble."

"Then you shouldn't have possessed Frank!" Sam drew his blessed letter opener from inside his jacket, shoved himself off the stairs, and lunged.

I grabbed for something, anything to block Sam's attack. My hand found a toner cartridge. I swung with all my might. The plastic connected firmly with Sam's wrist, diverting the blade.

Fluffy black powder exploded between us.

I scrambled up, coughing, and backed away. Sam wiped his face and stepped forward. Too late, I realized that I'd backed myself into the corner. I gripped the toner cartridge in two hands like a sword. A very short plastic sword. Oh, so intimidating.

"I'm not a demon," I said, and it was true. I was neither angel nor demon. Not anymore.

Sam sneered. "I'd expect a demon to say that."

He jabbed at me, and I batted his blade aside. More toner puffed out, but only a small cloud. Then Sam lunged, blade low, and I swung the cartridge downward. He shifted at the last moment, whipped the blade above my block, and stabbed it into my right shoulder.

The dull letter opener sank into muscle.

My scream echoed up the stairwell. I slapped at Sam's wrist. The blade yanked free, and I fell back against the wall. "That hurt!" I yelled, hand pressed to the wound.

At least the blessed blade hadn't banished me to Hell or separated my soul from Frank's body.

Sam backed away, eyes bright. "Frank? Is that you? Are you back?"

Frank's phone rang before I could answer. Sam and I stared at each other—him inquisitive, me furious—as the phone jingled cheerfully from my pocket. He gestured toward it.

Jaw clenched in pain, I yanked the phone free. This had better be Alvin with my key out of this bloody body! I couldn't take much more of being human.

I jabbed the ACCEPT button. "What?"

"Hi, I've been trying to reach you about your car's extended warranty."

Seriously? Why did I even bother answering?

"Now's really not a good time," I hissed through my teeth, eying Sam. He shifted his grip on the letter opener but didn't lower it.

"It's always a good time to save money!" that bloody mechanical voice said.

"I don't want to save money. I want you to go away."

"Our tow-away package is included!"

"No, not tow away ... *go away!*"

"A way to save money? Glad you asked!" My teeth ground. "All we need, Mr. Totmann, is—"

"I am not Frank Totmann! I am the Grim Reaper!" I bellowed into the phone and then hung up.

Sam's eyebrows creased, and his head cocked back. "Wait, what?"

I sighed. "I tried to tell you last time. I came to reap Frank Totmann's soul, but he tricked me, swapped our souls, and scurried off like a schoolyard bully, leaving me wasting away in this wreck of a body!"

Sam straightened and lowered the letter opener. "Really? Woah." The blade disappeared into his suit jacket. He tried brushing toner from his blue shirt sleeve, but it only smeared. "So, Frank cheated Death? Good for him."

"That's all you have to say? You stabbed me!"

Sam had the courtesy to look chagrined. "Sorry about that." He cocked his head to one side, eyes curious. "You're really the Grim Reaper?"

I drew a deep breath and grimaced at the pain in my shoulder. "Is that so hard to believe?"

Sam's lips pursed. "Considering what I've seen? I guess not." He eyed the blood seeping between my fingers. "Tell you what; let's get all this toner to my office, and I'll patch you up. Then, by way of apology, I'll treat you to a cup of coffee and you can tell me the whole story."

It didn't sound sufficient to make up for *stabbing me,* but I nodded and pushed away from the wall. "You have skills at binding wounds?"

He shook his head and gave an exaggerated sigh. "Everyone underestimates the supply guy! *Of course* I have skills at 'binding wounds.'" He said that last bit in a mocking tone and knelt to gather toner boxes.

"Noted," I said. I most certainly would not underestimate Samuel Davidson. I awkwardly retrieved a few boxes while keeping pressure on the wound and added them to the stack in Sam's arms. My shoulder throbbed. Finding allies among humanity was more difficult—and more painful—than I'd expected, but things were finally looking up.

Chapter 16

DEMON HUNTER

COFFEE AND DONUTS WERE apparently an IRS auditor's primary fuel. The small café on the first floor bustled with employees seeking their caffeine and sugar fix while ignoring work. Sam and I sat at a small table in the back corner. My back was to the wall, and I had an easy view of the hallway through the glass wall beside me. A muted television in the corner over the door played ongoing news coverage of the Cheer and Dance Nationals. Apparently, after the violence of the night before, the competition had been completely canceled. Now the teams were protesting outside some municipal building.

I shook my head. Humanity faced its greatest existential crisis in five thousand years and what were they worried about? Screaming teenage girls in glittery leotards. I would never understand humans.

But at least humanity had perfected the art of coffee. The black brew in my paper cup smelled divine. I took a sip. Warmth suffused my chest. Lovely, with a hint of bitter bite. It was almost enough to make me forgive Sam for stabbing me. Almost. My shoulder still throbbed despite two butterfly bandages, a nice padding of gauze, and 800mg of something called Motrin.

Sadly, Sam's skills ended with physical wounds. My brown tweed jacket now sported a large bloodstain around the puncture hole.

I took another sip and eyed Sam from across the small table. "I'll cut to the chase. I need your help. Frank Totmann swapped our souls with an ancient Sumerian spell, and I need to reverse that spell."

Sam's eyebrows rose, and he wrapped both hands around his paper coffee cup. "Not sure what you think I can do. I have a blessed blade and an open third eye, but that's it. Sumerian soul-swapping spells are way outside my wheelhouse."

"Perhaps, but you have other knowledge that may prove vital."

"Like what?" Sam sipped his coffee.

"You know Alvin Bureaucracy, head of Hell's Department of Bureaucratic Torments. He owes me a favor."

Sam hissed and made shushing motions. "Keep your voice down! The IRS may seem like a den of soulless auditors"—that sounded about right—"but nobody here *actually* has connections to the underworld."

"Except you."

"Not by choice."

"So, what is your connection to Alvin?"

Sam waved his hand dismissively. "That's between him and me. Bottom line, I may *know* Alvin, but we're not exactly friends."

I sat back and took another sip, intrigued. "Did you sell him your soul?"

A half-smile creased Sam's face. "Nah. Just a bit of my time."

"In Hell's service?"

"Sort of."

"Yet you banish demons."

"Yup."

"How did you acquire a blessed blade?"

"What's with the twenty questions?"

"I appreciate finding an ally, but you are a mystery. You have an open third eye, a blessed blade, and have admitted to some kind of business relationship with a senior demon. What are you, Samuel Davidson?"

He shrugged. "My wife Inez calls me a demon hunter, so that's as good a label as any. I don't hunt 'em by choice, mind you, but it helps me pass the time. She even helps sometimes."

A husband-and-wife demon-hunting team? Fascinating! "It's good to have a partner who supports you."

Sam's half-smile warmed. "Yeah. I really won the jackpot with Inez."

"Is your wife one of the faithful?"

Sam waggled his hand. "Sort of. She also believes in ghosts, vampires, Chupacabra, and any other nightmare you can imagine."

"Ah. A wise woman indeed."

Sam's coffee cup paused halfway to his lips. "Excuse me?"

"Nightmares are real, brought to life in Hell's sixth sub-level to torment the damned. Their incarnations, however, rarely make it into your world."

Sam's coffee cup resumed its journey, and he took a contemplative drink. "So, you ever have a partner? Someone to support you in your work?"

Wouldn't that be nice? To have someone share Death's burden. Evelyn might have been the one, but I didn't want to talk about her. I still couldn't believe I'd seen her in the basement. I took a swig of coffee to avoid answering and glanced at the muted television in the corner. A male reporter stood outside Wehling Memorial Hospital, wind whipping his hair. He looked grave. The banner at the bottom of the screen said, 'Coma Conundrum Continues.'

As if I needed the reminder that Frank wasn't doing his job. My job.

The door opened and Cora waltzed in with a jangle of jewelry, Elizabeth on her heels. Evelyn stalked protectively behind the intern, gaze sweeping the room.

I swore quietly into my coffee cup. Sam heard me and twisted in his chair, following my gaze. His eyebrows rose, and he turned back.

"Who's she?" he asked. I knew which *she* he was talking about. Sam had an open third eye, after all.

"Evelyn. She was my..." I choked on the words. My

what? Better half? Greatest regret? Seeing her again was like a spike twisting through my heart. "She was the one who supported me in my work," I said quietly. Cora and Elizabeth stepped to the counter and debated lattes and mochas. They didn't noticed me.

Evelyn did. She crossed her arms and stepped between Elizabeth and me. As if *I* were a threat.

Sam's lowered his voice to match mine. His whisper was barely audible over the espresso machine. "So, what happened between you two?"

"It was eons ago. I ... made a mistake, chose sides, and Evelyn paid the price."

Sam opened his mouth to respond but was interrupted by none other than Alvin Bureaucracy. Alvin slid through the glass wall next to us and hopped onto the little table, suit looking more rumpled than usual.

"There you are!" he said in his nasal whine, clawed finger pointed at me.

"Here *I am?* Where have *you* been?"

"You wouldn't believe what's going on! All Hell's broken loose. The Auditor knows you're gone, but not that you're Frank, and now—"

"Demon!" Evelyn's rough growl cut him off. All three

of us spun toward her. *Mercy* was bared, the curved black blade seeming to absorb the light. Evelyn's black wings snapped out like a wall between us and Elizabeth.

Alvin's beady red eyes bulged. "Oh, shit."

Evelyn's gaze flicked to me. "Consorting with the enemy, Grim?"

"They were never my enemies. A lot changed while you were gone."

"Evil hasn't." There was iron in her voice. Death in her eyes. She charged.

With a warbling high-pitched shriek, Alvin leapt from the table, barely avoiding Evelyn's lunging thrust. He scampered toward the espresso bar. Evelyn spun after him.

I jumped to my feet, sending my chair clattering to the floor. "Evelyn, stop!"

She ignored me. Alvin slid behind the espresso bar with Evelyn right behind him. He dashed between baristas while her wings pumped in the small space, giving her added speed.

Silence settled over the coffee shop. Silence, that is, aside from Alvin's terrified shrieks as he dodged around and through people and furniture. Nobody saw the spiritual battle raging around them. Every human gaze was fixed on me.

Damn.

Cora stood frozen halfway through handing the cashier her credit card. Her eyes narrowed. "Who is Evelyn?"

"She is ... not your concern." I kept my voice even, though my fists were clenched.

Alvin scrambled past a bakery display and shot through the café's door with Evelyn close behind. They disappeared into the hall, and silence settled once again.

Elizabeth leaned close to Cora and whispered. "Is Frank okay?"

Cora's lips pursed, and she turned back to the cashier. "Frank's ... not feeling like himself these days. Just ignore him."

Elizabeth shook her head at Cora and stepped over to me. I was so surprised at her approach that I froze like a rabbit. She placed a hand on my upper arm, and I felt that odd tingle again. Her emotions trickled into me, a wash of concern and compassion.

Good heavens, I was a fool not to see it before. Elizabeth was an empath! Though not as rare a gift as humans would like to believe, it wasn't exactly common. While I could read someone's soul like a book, she perceived emotions like an orchestral symphony dimly heard.

She leaned close, voice lowered for my ears alone. "Death is never the answer. I won't stand by again..." Elizabeth shook herself and drew a quick breath. "Before you do anything rash, talk to someone. You are not alone."

What? Oh! She thought I was suicidal. Were my emotions such a dark tangle? Hmmm. Perhaps. "Trust me," I whispered back, "though death is always on my mind, dying is the last thing I want to do." Especially after what I'd witnessed at Wehling Memorial last night. "Thank you for your concern."

She searched my eyes for a moment and gave the bloody stab wound in my jacket a pointed look before nodding and returning to Cora.

Activity in the coffee shop resumed, though more quietly than before. Furtive gazes flicked my way. I tried to ignore them and grabbed my coffee. Sam rose to join me and caught my gaze, seemingly as unsettled as I was. His hand was inside his jacket, no doubt gripping *Faith*.

I drew a deep breath and blew it out. "I need to leave."

"Back to your office?" he asked.

"No. The Auditor knows I'm gone, and his minions are already hunting Frank." I realized that I hadn't told

Sam about the Auditor yet, so I explained. "The Auditor is Hell's final arbiter of the Rules. He's a snake who has always coveted my position as Death."

Sam shrugged. "He didn't seem that bad to me."

My jaw dropped a little. "You know *the Auditor?*"

"I *may* have helped Alvin pull one over on the old goat."

I realized that my jaw was still hanging open, and I clicked it shut. I retrieved my chair and sat. "You deceived The Auditor? And your soul survived intact?" I eyed Sam with newfound respect as he rejoined me at the table.

"He never found out. Good thing too. The Auditor seemed like quite the stickler for the rules."

"You mean the Rules."

Sam frowned. "That's what I said."

"No, you didn't give the Rules the proper emphasis. The proper respect. They aren't like rules in a child's game that might be changed or ignored at a whim. These are the Rules that govern everything within the spiritual realm. The Rules even govern me, the Reaper. Spirits are bound to the Rules so fully that we *cannot* violate them." I kept my voice low, but despite a few residual glances from my outburst, nobody was close enough to hear us.

Cora and Elizabeth had occupied a table in the cafe's

far corner, under the television. As far away from me as possible, I was sure, though Elizabeth kept glancing my way.

Sam toyed with his cup. "So, it's like the Ten Commandments? Thou shalt not murder and all that?"

"More like, 'Thou shalt not interfere with Death's duties,' and 'Thou shalt not violate human free will.' Even banishing demons with your blessed letter opener is governed by the Rules. Blessed blades send demons to Hell and cursed blades send angels to Heaven. Returning to the mortal realm after a banishment takes significant time and effort."

Sam snorted. "Unless you're Alvin Bureaucracy. That little weasel bounced back twenty-four hours after I banished him."

"After you ... what? When did this happen?"

Sam waved his hand dismissively. "Long story, water under the bridge at this point."

I pursed my lips. Sam was entirely too cagey about his past. He continued.

"So, if the Rules are so strict, then how'd you end up like this?" He waved at Frank's corpulent body. I grimaced.

"There are loopholes. Frank found one with his Sumerian spell. I need to close it."

Evelyn slid back through the wall by Cora and Elizabeth's table. Her arms were crossed, and her glower was fierce.

I breathed a sigh of relief. "Alvin survived."

Sam quirked a smile. "Never doubted him. That little worm could survive Armageddon."

"I've tarried too long." I rose again, and Sam joined me.

"Where will you go?"

"I don't know, but I can't return to Frank's life. The Auditor and his minions can track me through his connections." I strode for the door, purposely avoiding Evelyn's gaze. Cora and Elizabeth watched me leave with matching worried frowns.

Sam followed me, looking thoughtful. We stepped into the hall, and he said, "Come to my house."

"What?"

"Frank and I aren't friends, so there's no reason for the Auditor to look for you there. You can lay low while we try to find Alvin again."

I frowned. "I couldn't impose."

"No imposition. Besides, I still owe you for the whole stabbing thing."

I nodded. "True. Thank you, I gratefully accept."

Sam grinned, a bounce lightening his step. "Inez is going to *flip* when I tell her that the Grim Reaper is coming to dinner!"

I grimaced but said nothing. It was embarrassing to be reduced from 'the terror of men's souls' to 'quirky dinner guest,' but I'd accept the ignominy if it got me out of here and away from the Auditor's minions. I'd had enough brushes with my own mortality for one day.

Chapter 17

THE IMMORTAL

SAM LIVED IN A modest two-story house at the south end of Colorado Springs. It was one of those communities where every house looked like its neighbor and streets were named things like 'Forest Grove' and 'Shadow Brook.' I saw no forests nor brooks on our drive, just carbon-copy suburbia.

Sam parked in the driveway, and we entered through the front door. The entry led into a tiled hallway with carpeted stairs climbing to our left, a dining room to our right, and a combined kitchen and living room at the end of the hall. The ceilings were high enough that even the Auditor could have stridden through the house without stooping.

An excited shriek sounded from the kitchen followed by a small child in a pink tutu and a foam knight's helmet.

"Daddy!"

The little ballerina-knight bowled into Sam's legs. He stumbled back, almost knocking me back out the open door. "What are you doing home?" he asked. "I thought the preschool bus picked you up at noon?"

A woman's voice yelled from the kitchen. "Beatrix was running a fever this morning, so I told the school I'd keep her home this afternoon."

"She seems fine to me." Sam shuffled aside enough to let me close the door. Beatrix merely tightened her grip, burrowing into his legs.

There was an exasperated sigh from the kitchen, and something clanged into the sink. "Tell me about it. Your daughter's driving me nuts!"

"Hey, she gets her energy from *your* side of the family." Sam knelt to peel his daughter off his legs. He held her at arm's length and removed her helmet to reveal lively blue eyes and a rat's nest of brown hair. A line of green goo ran from Beatrix's nose across her cheek. Like she'd half-heartedly wiped it after sneezing inside her helmet.

Sam made a terrified face. "Gah! It's a monster! Who are you, and what have you done with my daughter?" The little girl giggled, roared with convincing ferocity, then tore out of his grip to bolt up the stairs. Hands and feet pattered the carpeted treads before a door upstairs slammed shut.

Sam's wife strode from the kitchen, wiping her hands on a towel. She was taller than Sam with short, fiery red hair and mismatched green and blue eyes. Unlike Cora's clattering jangle of jewelry, Inez only wore a simple wedding ring on one hand balanced by a woven gold band on her other. "Why are *you* home? It's barely lunch..." She trailed off when she saw me, and her eyebrows rose in surprise.

I gazed deep into her mismatched eyes and read her soul. Inez Davidson, thirty-seven years old, death in ... what?

My breath caught. I read her again.

Inez had no date of death. Not a variable date ... no date. I'd never seen that before. Was I losing my powers?

Sam smiled at his wife. "Inez, I'd like you to meet Grim."

Inez shook my hand with a calloused grip. "I assume that's a last name. As in 'Brothers Grimm?'"

"No," I said. "As in 'The Grim Reaper.'"

She snorted. "I deserved that. Welcome, Grim. What brings you to our house in the middle of the day?"

"I am on the run, and your husband offered sanctuary."

The amusement drained from Inez's face. She glanced at Sam, then back at me. "Okay," she said. "Looks like I have some catching up to do. You two can fill me in over lunch. I hope you like leftover pizza."

"Sounds marvelous," I said and followed Inez, the first immortal human I'd ever met, into the kitchen. Curiosity burned inside me.

***

I didn't tell my tale immediately. Mundane details had to be addressed first. Like heating the pizza and distracting the child with the television. My tale was not one for innocent ears.

Beatrix popped in to roar at us again, this time wearing a convincing dragon costume that looked like it had been fashioned out of a dark green hoodie. Glittery felt wings were attached to her arms and floppy horns adorned the hood.

Sam screamed in dutiful terror before setting her up in the living room with a movie, cheese pizza, and a pile of napkins I doubted she'd use.

The shag-carpeted living room and tiled kitchen were one large rectangular space separated by a couch that faced the television. From what I could see of the screen, Beatrix's cartoon involved lots of singing by a girl wearing blue, bumbling fairies, and a villain in purple and black who was all pointy edges.

The rest of us ate our pizza at the kitchen island where Inez could keep an eye on her messy child. It was difficult to concentrate over the sounds of animated song, dance, and mayhem, but I did my best and told Inez my tale of becoming human.

She didn't interrupt me once, though her blue and green eyes often widened in disbelief. Yet her incredulity faded as I continued. I finished my story along with my third slice of pepperoni, and Inez shook her head in surprise.

"The Grim Reaper, trapped in a human body. Wild! You don't have any powers?"

"I can still read human souls through their eyes, and other spirits can read my soul, but that's all." I didn't mention the mystery of Inez's soul. I checked it again through her eyes, but the answer remained unchanged. She had no date of death.

Sam pointed his pizza slice at me. "So, what happens if

you don't swap souls again with Frank?"

"The end of life as you know it."

His face scrunched up. "Come on, isn't that a bit dramatic?"

"Humans have an allotted time upon this earth. Some longer, some shorter, but everyone dies." I pointed at the television where the heroine was climbing a dark, foreboding stairwell while orchestral music built tension. "If you switched your television to the news, you would hear stories of miraculous recoveries. Of people who should have died, but their spirits continue to hang on."

Inez nodded. "The radio said something about the Coma Conundrum this morning. There was a big pile-up on I-25 last night, but nobody died despite some horrific injuries. Instead, half of the injured went into a coma instead."

Sam shrugged. "So, what's the problem? Sounds like surviving calamities is a good thing."

I shook my head at his short-sightedness. "There is a reason the body ceases to function at certain thresholds. Yes, they went into a coma, but they still feel pain. Those survivors are, right now, suffering unimaginable agony. Pain that the human psyche is not meant to endure because they're supposed to be *dead*, their souls moved on."

"So ... Frank's not doing your job right, and the world suffers?"

"Precisely." The cartoon's music echoed through the shared space with a crescendo that ended with a crash of symbols. I tapped the kitchen island. "That's why I need to reverse Frank's spell. Alvin was looking into it for me, but Evelyn chased him away before he could tell me what he found."

"What about Cora?" Inez asked. "She provided the ingredients for the spell. Surely, she could dig up something about reversing it."

I shook my head. "Cora won't help me. She's on Frank's side, proud of him for cheating death. I tried to explain the problem, but she wouldn't listen."

Sam swallowed his last bite and wiped his hands on a napkin. "What about Heaven? You've been focused on Hell and demons, why not ask the other side for help? Surely, they'd be interested in getting you your powers back."

I drew a deep breath and shook my head. "The Almighty has His own inscrutable priorities. I refuse to talk to Gabriel"—not after he'd forced me to abandon

Evelyn at Megiddo—"and most other angels won't talk to *me*. They consider me a traitor for my part in the Fall."

"The what?" Sam tossed his napkin in the trash under the sink.

"You know the story: Adam and Eve eating from the forbidden Tree of the Knowledge of Good and Evil?"

"Sure."

"That was Lucifer who tricked them. The Devil himself. My part came years later with their sons. I—" My throat closed. I'd never admitted my original sin aloud before. I glanced at Sam and Inez. Could I share my dark past?

Animated lightning on the television struck with a boom that made me jump. I drew a deep breath and squared my shoulders. I'd given the Davidsons my trust, may as well give them my confession. In for a penny, in for a pound.

"I was the one who convinced Cain to kill Abel. I was trying to prove a point to the Auditor about humanity's innate goodness. Cain proved me wrong, and I introduced mankind to murder."

As if on cue, the cartoon villain roared with maniacal laughter as the deep music swelled yet again.

"Oh, God." Inez's hand flew to her mouth. "But that

was forever ago."

"True," I said, "but we spirits don't forget. Forgiveness is hard earned and hard given. That's one reason for the complete polarization of the spiritual war. Pure evil against pure good. I stand in the middle, no longer an angel, but not quite a demon. I am simply ... Death." A deep sigh escaped me. "At least, I was."

Inez placed a comforting hand on my wrist. "Is there no one who will listen to you?"

I shrugged. "Gabriel and I haven't talked in millennia. I doubt he'd help me. Even though he was instrumental in turning me into the Grim Reaper, he never liked the idea of granting me *Grace*." I glanced up and saw my hosts' confused expressions. "My scythe. Forged in the fires of Hell and blessed by the Almighty, three blades were created even before the Rules were established: *Grace*, *Mercy*, and *Justice*. My scythe *Grace* was designed to impart balance. When I reap a soul, it goes to Purgatory to await the balancing of scales, the Judgment of one's choices against an eternity of blessing or an eternity of suffering."

"Who holds the other blades?" Sam asked.

Inez added, "And what do they do?"

"Gabriel holds *Justice*, wielding it on behalf of the

Almighty. To be struck by *Justice* is to be judged immediately. You bypass Purgatory and get dropped straight into the Lake of Fire. *Justice* has only been used once, to cast Lucifer himself from Heaven. Gabriel holds it for the day of Armageddon."

Inez shuddered and withdrew the hand she'd placed on my wrist. Her mismatched eyes looked troubled. "And *Mercy*? Does that send souls to heaven?"

My jaw clenched. "No. It's not that kind of mercy. It unmakes a soul, ending it forever. No eternal blessings and no eternal suffering. *Mercy* delivers a true death. It is the most powerful of the three blades, but I'd thought it lost until today." I eyed Sam. "Evelyn carries *Mercy*, the black blade of unmaking."

"Woah." He ran his fingers through his brown hair. "Alvin's lucky he escaped her."

"Indeed. But whatever knowledge he may have found is lost to me now. Alvin Bureaucracy is many things, but brave is nowhere on that list—"

"True." Sam's chuckle was wry.

"—so, he is likely hiding somewhere dark and inaccessible. Out of my reach. I need some other way of reversing Frank's spell, but at this point I have ... nothing."

Inez and Sam exchanged glances before Inez said, "Whenever I have a problem I can't solve, I step back for a while. Inspiration can't be forced, so let your subconscious gnaw on the details while you do something else."

"Like what?"

"Something mundane. That's when I usually get my best inspirations. When I'm not trying to force things but let my mind rest and wander."

I cocked an eyebrow. "Death does not rest," I said, but then considered Alvin's incessant needs. I was human now, and the body needed rest to function. The mind was part of the body. My compounding problems flitted through my mind. Frank's spell, the Auditor and his minions, Evelyn's return with her burning anger, and even the mystery of Sam's past and Inez's future all vied for dominance, each problem begging for solutions and making my skull feel like a pot about to boil over. Inez was right. I shook my head and sighed. "Oh, very well."

She nodded as if my acquiescence had been a foregone conclusion.

We fell into contemplative silence as Beatrix's cartoon resolved its plotlines with happy song and dance, the villain destroyed, and the princess saved.

If only real life were so simple.

Chapter 18

MUNDANE NOVELTY

THE REMAINDER OF WEDNESDAY, my third day as a human, was one of mundane novelty. Sam returned to the Land of Evil Auditors—unlike Frank, he wasn't senior enough to disappear without telling anyone—and I spent the afternoon with Inez and Beatrix.

Inez, I learned, was a certified nurse who worked part-time at an assisted living facility. I too had spent much time in such facilities, so we had an enjoyable conversation on the couch about end-of-life care.

Beatrix, as I suspected was the case with most children, was enthusiastic about everything except naptime. It was amusing to watch the little dragon argue that she was *not* tired despite several betraying yawns. She shook her head so fiercely that the droopy horns slapped her lightly on the forehead. Beatrix crossed her arms, refusing to budge from the living room until *I* read her a story.

Inez shook her head. "You can't demand stories from everyone you meet!"

I held up a forestalling hand. "I would be delighted. My time with children is usually limited and sad"—Death visits entirely too many children—"so this is a pleasant change from the norm."

Inez's forehead wrinkled until understanding lit her eyes. Her expression softened, and she nodded to Beatrix. "One story, then upstairs young lady."

Beatrix beamed at having gotten her way and scrambled to a little bookshelf under the window to my right. She retrieved a board book and thrust it at me with a grin before snuggling up with her mother on the couch.

I opened the book and read.

Click, Clack, Moo: Cows that Type by Doreen Cronin was, by far, the most ridiculous story imaginable. Cow hooves are entirely the wrong shape for a typewriter's keys! Conniving chickens and ducks I understood—humans often underestimate the fowl fiends—but I've never known cows to express even the slightest interest in type-written correspondence.

Utterly preposterous!

Regardless, Beatrix was enthralled. She giggled maniacally throughout the story and gave a convincing 'moooooo' at every appropriate opportunity.

I ended *Click, Clack, Moo* to gales of laughter from my audience. Perhaps the ridiculous nature of the story was the entire point. I couldn't help but smile. A child's laughter was not something I often heard in my line of work. Perhaps I could offer a story to the next child I reap. A bit of levity to ease their transition.

If I ever resumed my mantle as Death.

"Again!" Beatrix demanded, flipping back to page one.

"No!" Inez said, but then Frank's phone rang.

My shoulders tensed. This better not be that eternally accursed extended warranty machine! I tried to ignore the phone, but it just kept ringing, so I dug it out of my pocket. I answered tentatively.

"Hello?"

"Hi, I've been trying to reach you about your car's extended warranty."

"I knew it! Why don't you go bother someone else, you mechanical misfit of a telemarketer?"

Beatrix's eyes lit up, and she snatched the phone from me. I was too surprised to react as she put it to her ear. Her voice became deathly quiet and earnest.

"Hello..."

Even I could barely hear her breathy whisper. Utterly confused, I glanced at Inez, who hid a laugh behind her hand. She whispered, "We always give Beatrix the phone when telemarketers call."

I blinked at her, then sat back to listen to the most bizarre one-sided conversation of my life.

"Fiona the Sparkly Fairy," Beatrix said, maintaining her intense whisper.

"Blue."

"Four."

"Cookies!" That came out with a yell and a smile.

"They're busy."

"Only *death*." This was again low and earnest. My eyebrows shot up while Inez snorted.

"One *billion* dollars!"

"No."

There was a long silence as Beatrix listened, occasionally

nodding into the phone before she said, "Okay. Bubye!" She handed the phone back to me. The telemarketer was gone.

"Thank you," I told her sincerely. Beatrix beamed and grabbed *Click, Clack, Moo* again, but Inez scooped her up off the couch.

"Oh, no! It's nap time, young lady. You got an extra three minutes with the telemarketer. Say thank you for the story."

"Thank you!" Beatrix said, and Inez carried her upstairs.

A few minutes later, Inez returned, looking pleased. "That was kind of you to read to Beatrix," she said, dropping onto the couch. "Thank you."

I returned the book to its shelf and rejoined Inez on the couch. "I have limited experience with fiction. None, really, before yesterday. I was watching a television program called *Another Day in Paradise* when—"

Inez squeaked like a little girl and covered her mouth.

I froze, surprised at her reaction. I cocked an eyebrow and said, "I take it you watch *Another Day*?"

Inez composed herself and folded her hands in her lap, but her eyes shone. "Don't tell Sam. It's my guilty pleasure. He thinks soap operas are ridiculous, and they are, but I can't get enough of *Another Day in Paradise*." She leaned forward. "I think Felicity needs to ditch Edward—"

"Edward?"

"The silver fox she's dating."

"Ah."

"—but there's no chance of a reunion with Mario. Not after what he did last week."

My brows furrowed. "Last week?"

Inez's mouth formed a perfect O as her eyebrows shot up. "You don't know? When did you start watching?"

"Just yesterday."

"Oh, there's so much I need to tell you!"

And that's what she did. For the next half-hour, Inez indoctrinated me into the mind-boggling intricacies of *Another Day in Paradise*'s fictional relationships. I couldn't untangle them all, but that was okay. Through our discussion, I learned several interesting facts unrelated to the television program.

First, Inez was a hopeless romantic and an optimist who swept me up with her enthusiasm. She'd met and married the man she loved in her early twenties and believed to her core that true love was real. It was a touching sentiment, if a bit naïve. I'd seen the end results of love gone terribly wrong too often.

Yet, at the same time, I'd also seen old married couples who had died within minutes of each other because their hearts could not stand the separation. So, perhaps her opinion had some validity. She and Sam seemed to have a solid relationship, from what I'd seen in my admittedly short acquaintance with them.

Second—and this was the more important observation—Inez was normal. As normal as a woman could be. She had hopes and fears, passions and frustrations. Listening to her gush about fictional characters told me a lot about her core beliefs.

And it told me *nothing* about what I wanted to know.

Why the *hell* did Inez Davidson not have a known date of death?

Unfortunately, I couldn't ask her. The living aren't meant to know their date of death. It's one of the Rules. Regardless, immortality for the human body is impossible without direct intervention from either Heaven or Hell. The first humans did live inordinately long lives compared to modern humanity—measured in centuries instead of decades—but they still died.

I know. I was there for each and every one.

Yet Inez was not someone whom I could see Heaven or Hell deeming worthy of immortality. She was not of the faithful, though she believed some interesting things that made even my eyebrows arch, and she was not a servant of Lucifer. She was simply ... a woman. No more, no less.

It was immensely frustrating.

Inez glanced at her watch.

"So," she said, "do you want to watch *Another Day?* We should have just enough time to finish before Beatrix wakes up from her nap."

I nodded, and she turned on the television. For the next hour, we sat in comfortable silence, living vicariously through fiction. It was, perhaps, the most enjoyable hour I'd had since becoming human. On par with my dinner with Cora, certainly.

It took me a while to realize that it wasn't the events themselves that I appreciated, but the companionship of enjoying something together with a friend.

I'd never had many friends; none among humans.

Beatrix thundered downstairs not long after the show ended, and the afternoon suddenly became louder and more exciting. A mundane afternoon, yet novel to my experience.

I began to see why humans clung to life so tenaciously.

Chapter 19

THE GATES OF ABADDON

THAT NIGHT I DREAMED. It was a new experience for me; dreaming is a human conceit. I don't know why my subconscious chose *this* night to rifle my memories, but it did. I recognized the memory in this dream, though I'd tried hard to forget it.

I stood upon a cliff edge above the valley of Megiddo, looking down upon the carnage of a battle soon to end. The entire Heavenly Host waited with me in the blazing sunlight, standing silent and stiff along the ridgeline. Angels watched men getting slaughtered. They didn't interfere, awaiting Gabriel's signal.

Chaos reigned in the valley below us. I would like to say that Death reigned below, but I stayed where I was as men from the land of Ur fought an army of demons and half-demon spawn.

The Urites were losing. Badly.

These were the days of the Nephilim, giant abominations born after demons bred with humanity over five thousand years ago. Yet not all the half-human demon-spawn became Nephilim. A few, perhaps a hundred all told, became something more. Demigods. Flesh made immortal, imbued with demonic power, and pure evil. The Demigods had in turn spawned a dark army of Cambion, mindless beasts who were more than human yet so much less.

I eyed the Heavenly Host. Anger and frustration filled angelic faces as they watched the carnage. None bore swords or spears, only stout staves. The only swords among the Host were Gabriel's *Justice* and Evelyn's *Mercy*. Gabriel stood at my side, Evelyn just beyond him.

No, Gabriel didn't stand *at* my side. That makes it sound as though we were partners. Friends. We were—*are*—anything but. We merely stood near each other. My gaze flicked to Evelyn on Gabriel's far side; his captain and the only reason I'd agreed to come.

She looked magnificent, resplendent in white leather armor that offset her dark skin and black wings. Her hair shone like the night sky, tied in intricate braids that formed a tight crown before flowing down her back.

Of all the Heavenly Host, only Evelyn still accepted me. Still smiled at me. I had loved her once, back when I too had been an angel.

She had loved me too, I think.

But today was not about lost love. Today was about the war between good and evil, between Heaven and Hell. I shifted my skeletal feet, edging toward the cliff. I should be down there reaping the souls of the slain.

Gabriel cocked an eyebrow at me. "You can parse souls later, Grim." His voice was deep and melodic. A bass that commanded respect, regardless of whether I wanted to give it. "I need you here."

I whirled on him, my bony brow ridges furrowed. Fire crackled in my empty eye sockets. "Why ask me to attend a massacre if I'm not supposed to do my job? You strain my impartiality to the limit. Your fight with Hell is not mine.

Not anymore."

A shadow passed across Gabriel's face. "I do not wish the Urites to suffer, but I cannot risk a live human being dragged into Abaddon."

"Abaddon? *That's* why you called me here?"

"You hold the key to Abaddon. Only you can open it." He pointed at *Grace*, and I rocked back on my heels, clutching the scythe. "We're going to send these demons and the abominations they created into the realm of eternal darkness."

"Abaddon is for Lucifer alone!" I said, "*If* he loses at Armageddon. *This* is not the final battle. Lucifer and the Almighty aren't even here!"

"I know!" Gabriel glared at me. "But we will never reach Armageddon if the Nephilim and Demigods destroy mankind first. Look at them! At their rate of conquest, at their rate of *forced breeding,* no pure human souls will remain within a few generations. Only Cambion abominations. Hell will win before Armageddon even begins. And who will suffer the most? Humanity. Wiped out by forces they don't understand because Hell decided to cheat."

I turned to the battle. I was beholden to neither Heaven nor Hell, but to the humans whose souls were in my care.

The last knot of Urites fought valiantly against the dark army. The men cried to the heavens for salvation. They could not see the Heavenly Host; did not know that salvation had been withheld.

I felt when the last Urite died. Hundreds of souls screamed for release from this mortal coil, the weight of their need pulling at me. Without me there to reap them, these souls would remain trapped within dead and devastated bodies. Wracked with pain and fully aware of the horrors surrounding them, but unable to do anything.

A shiver writhed through my bones.

A raucous cheer rose from the dark army. The Nephilim and Demigods *could* see the Heavenly Host, and they jeered and spat lewd curses at us. The demons among them cackled, drunk on bloodlust.

With clenched jaws, I turned to Gabriel. "The last Urite is dead."

"Open the Gates of Abaddon," he said, then gestured to Evelyn. "Go."

She smiled at me—a fierce warrior's smile tinged with sorrow at the massacre we'd just witnessed. She raised *Mercy,* the curved blade a slice of pure darkness in the sunlight.

"For Heaven!" she called and leapt from the cliff, midnight wings spread wide. A war cry rose from the Heavenly Host, and ten thousand angels swept into the valley, staves in hand.

I understood now why they'd left their swords behind. Heavenly blades would merely banish a demon—or its spawn—to Hell's upper levels. Banished spirits could and would eventually return to the mortal realm. Similarly, a demonic blade would banish an Angel to Heaven.

None would return from Abaddon. This was eternal damnation served early and Heaven couldn't afford for any to escape by simply being banished to Hell's upper levels.

I twisted my scythe's handle, stopped time, and slammed *Grace*'s blade into the cliff below my feet. A crack sundered earth and stone, racing down the cliff face until it hit the valley. It broke left and right along the base of the cliff and split wide into a gaping maw of darkness a hundred paces wide and five hundred long. The black void seemed to absorb all light.

The Gates of Abaddon were open.

Heaven's forces slammed into the dark army. The clash of bodies and the screams of rage rolled over me like thunder. The dark army surged away from Abaddon and fought with the ferocity of caged animals. Winged demons tried to escape, to fly to freedom, but angels broke from the main force and chased them down.

The battle did not end quickly. Demigods and demons with cursed blades struck down angels, banishing them from the mortal realm. Giant Nephilim fought with clubs and fists, screaming wordless rage as they pummeled any who dared approach. Yet, the Heavenly Host pressed forward, violence and overwhelming numbers slowly pushing the ravening horde toward Abaddon. It took time—though I'd made time stand still—but eventually the first Cambion slipped over the edge and fell screaming into Hell's deepest pit.

Evelyn fought at the forefront, *Mercy* sweeping before her. Demigods, demons, and Nephilim fought her and died, unraveling on her blade. Victims of *Mercy*'s true death. Only they would escape eternity in Abaddon.

A lone Demigod stood his ground at the edge of Abaddon's gates. Nigel, King of the Demigods, stood head and shoulders above the wretched creatures surrounding him. He looked human but fought like a titan, the strokes of his sword powerful and brutal.

Evelyn reached him. Their blades clashed with a crackle

of lightning. They fought fiercely, neither giving ground. Evelyn dodged, blocked, and counter-attacked, but she could not push him any further toward the pit.

Perhaps I could make the pit come to her.

I concentrated on *Grace*, forcing my will through the scythe. Abaddon fought me like a living thing, struggling against the wound I'd rent in its flesh. But I was stronger than eternal darkness.

I was Death incarnate.

The edge of the pit dropped away below Nigel's feet, the earth crumbling into inky blackness.

The King of the Demigods fell.

Nigel screamed and caught the pit's edge. His sword spiraled into the darkness.

Evelyn stalked forward; her blade lowered toward Nigel's throat. She said something I could not hear. Around her, the Heavenly Host pushed the last of the dark army into Abaddon. The screams of the damned faded into nothingness.

"Close it!" Gabriel yelled, his voice echoing into the valley.

Evelyn glanced up.

That was all it took.

In her moment of distraction, Nigel surged upward past *Mercy* and grabbed Evelyn's wrist. He tried to climb over her to escape Abaddon, but Evelyn slipped, overbalanced by his weight. She fell bodily into him, and together they tumbled, fighting, screaming into Abaddon's eternal darkness.

"No!" My concentration wavered and Abaddon shuddered, rough pit edges pulling together. I sent a surge of pure willpower and stopped them, keeping the gates open.

"Close it." Gabriel's voice was pained and quiet.

"But Evelyn..."

"It is done. You cannot save her without releasing these abominations into the world again. Better to lose one angel than all of mankind."

My shoulders hunched.

I couldn't do it. I couldn't trap the only soul I'd ever loved with the darkest evils Hell had ever devised.

But I had to. For humanity. Heaven help me, I had to abandon Evelyn. I yanked my scythe from the earth.

The Gates of Abaddon slammed shut.

***

I would like to say that I surged awake, screaming in agony at the memory of Evelyn's loss. But the anguish in my soul was too deep for that. I lay in the darkness of Sam and Inez's guest room, clutching the blanket around my shoulders, stifling the sobs that shook me.

More memories came, unbidden. Heaven and Hell had parlayed after Megiddo, each side blaming the other for going too far in their battle for men's souls. Thus were the Rules created. Limits placed upon every spirit, written upon their very souls, to ensure that such excesses never happened again.

A realization dawned on me, and I caught my breath. Evelyn was trapped in Abaddon during the parlay. She'd never been bound to the Rules. She was free, free as no other angel or demon was.

And she still had *Mercy*, the blade of unmaking.

An idea began to form. I still hadn't solved my soul-swapping problem with Frank, but perhaps I could solve my Auditor problem. Stop the hunt for me so that I could track down Frank. Evelyn and *Mercy* were the key—if I could convince her to help. It was a desperate gamble, but I was getting desperate.

I needed to kill the Auditor.

Chapter 20

EVELYN'S SMILE

THURSDAY BEGAN WITH SNOT and a story. I was jolted awake by a spray of mucus on my cheek followed by a sniffle. I lunged back, my shoulders hit the wall, and I scrubbed at my face. My hands came away wet and slimy. Mucus stuck to my beard.

Beatrix stood at the edge of my bed, a bubble of snot on her nose, staring with sleepy eyes and tousled brown hair that looked like a bird had nested in it. A stuffed red dragon dangled in a chokehold under one arm. She sniffled again, pulling the snot bubble back into her nose.

I stared back, unsure what to say.

Beatrix wiped her nose with the sleeve of her sparkly princess pajamas and blinked sleepily at me.

"Good morning, Beatrix," I said, sitting up and casting about for something to wipe my hands and face. Not finding anything readily handy, I used the sheets. "What time is it?"

She shrugged, her piercing blue eyes fixed on mine. Dim morning light shone through thin curtains, illuminating the right side of her face, and leaving the rest in shadows. Just past dawn, I guessed. Muted voices from the kitchen downstairs told me that I was the last to wake.

I leaned back against the wall. Pulling the blankets over my lap, I eyed my snot-filled little alarm clock.

"Aren't you supposed to be in bed?"

She squeezed her stuffed dragon and said, "Not tired."

"So, you decided that nobody should be sleeping?" Annoyance tinged my voice, and I scrubbed at my eyes.

Beatrix shrank in on herself. I sighed, feeling a spike of guilt for my tone. She was just a child curious about the stranger in her house. I didn't appreciate my rude awakening, but that was no reason to make her feel bad about herself. I drew a deep breath and blew it out.

"I'm sorry," I said. "I shouldn't have snapped. What

brings you here on such a gloriously *early* morning?"

"Tell me a story?"

"What kind of a story?"

She shrugged again.

My lips pursed. Reading to her yesterday had been enjoyable, but *telling* a story? How would that work? I couldn't lie!

Those big blue eyes stared up at me, pleading.

Oh, what the hell. Why not? I leaned forward. "Do you know who I am?"

Beatrix shook her head.

"I am"—I spread my arms for dramatic effect—"the Grim Reaper."

Her brows furrowed, and that snot bubble appeared again. "Who?"

I slumped back, deflated. "What? You've never heard of me?"

She shook her head, making her hairy bird's nest bobble.

"I am Death."

Her eyes widened.

"Ah, you know what that means."

"Grampa died." She pulled the stuffed dragon up to half-shield her face.

"I'm sorry for your loss, but that is the fate of all humankind." Except for her mother, a mystery that still bothered me. "But this story is not a story about death, but about love." I raised an eyebrow. "Do you like love stories?"

Beatrix's head nodded so fiercely that the bird's nest fell across her face, coming partially untangled. Between it and the dragon, all I saw of her was a single fixated eye.

"I was not always the Grim Reaper. Back in the days of old, when the earth was young and humanity was fresh and new, I was an angel."

That single eye bulged, and I smiled.

"I was not in this flaccid form you see before you." I waved a hand at Frank's body. "I was tall and proud with powerful golden wings." My hands spread wide in a mimicry of a wingspan. "And, most important to our story today, I was in love with an angel name Evelyn."

The stuffed-dragon-shield lowered, and Beatrix crawled halfway onto the edge of the bed.

"Courtship among angels is a serious matter. They do not wed in the same manner as humans, but some still choose a partner to spend eternity with. I was courting Evelyn and let me tell you"—I leaned forward conspiratorially—"she wasn't making it easy. But she was worth it.

"Evelyn was dark and fierce. Captain of the Heavenly Host, but with a delightful sense of humor. I was but a lowly guardian angel. My charge—" I paused. My charge was Cain, who became humanity's first murderer. Perhaps best not to mention those details with a four-year-old. I waved a hand. "Never mind. That's not important to the story. What *is* important is that I had planned a special night for Evelyn. The night I would ask her to spend eternity with me."

A tiny gasp escaped Beatrix, and she crawled the rest of the way onto the bed. She lay down and put her head on my shin, as though it were a pillow, her toy dragon clutched tightly in her arms.

"Evelyn loved waterfalls, and we'd visited every waterfall on Earth that we could find. The world was young and untamed in those days, and I found the perfect spot for us. A hidden gem that, so far as I could tell, neither human nor angelic eye had ever seen before, deep in the heart of what is now called Asia.

"Lush forest surrounded us, rich with the cries of birds and monkeys. We walked together under dense canopy until we came upon a river. As was our habit on these excursions, we had turned corporeal—taking physical form—so that we could fully experience the vibrant life surrounding us. I had prepared a raft for our adventure, a simple thing of logs bound with vines. We climbed aboard and pushed off from the shore."

Motion caught my eye, and I glanced up. Inez leaned against the doorframe, her short red hair a slightly less frazzled mess than her daughter's. She smiled at Beatrix's back and motioned for me to continue.

"Placid waters flowed beneath us, carrying our raft slowly downstream. Evelyn sat at my side, one knee up, the other leg trailing her bare foot in the water. She plucked flowers from low branches, smiling as she inhaled their fragrant aromas.

"And that is when it happened—"

Beatrix's eyes widened.

"A great lizard's snout burst from the water!" I clapped my hands, and Beatrix squeaked.

"A gharial, the long-nosed crocodile! Powerful jaws snapped at Evelyn's bare feet. She pulled her toes back just in time. The gharial slipped back into the water.

"Evelyn spun toward me, surprise and anger in her eyes. 'Is this the new adventure you promised? Getting eaten?'

"'No!' I said. But before I could say more, the gharial struck again, this time flinging half its body onto our raft."

I lowered my voice to a whisper. "The great lizard might have gotten us right then, but for one saving grace … I was terrible at tying knots."

Beatrix giggled and Inez smiled, crossing her arms.

"The raft split apart under the gharial's weight, throwing us into the river. We could have turned back into spirits at any point but experiencing life's wonders—and its dangers—was the whole reason we took these little adventures.

"Down we fell into the dark water, wings caught by the rushing currents that flowed beneath the river's placid surface. We swam as fast as we could underwater—angel wings are surprisingly helpful for swimming—before turning back toward our attacker. Through the dark water, we saw the gharial writhing, tangled in the vines from our raft. It spun, snapped, and tore at its bindings until it came free. The beast eyed us then, clearly considering whether we were worth the effort to chase down for a snack, then turned and swam languidly back upriver.

"What happened next, I'm sad to say, came as a surprise to me, even though it was part of my plan for the evening.

We were still underwater when a roaring filled our ears. It was muted, as all sounds are muted underwater, but Evelyn and I kicked for the surface as hard as we could. We broke free, drew deep breaths, and what do you think we saw when we looked downriver?"

"A dragon!" Beatrix said, thrusting her toy at me with a roar. I laughed and shook my head.

"No, worse. The river disappeared before us, falling away into a great hole in the forest floor. Evelyn barely had a chance to yell before we tumbled over a high waterfall that cut through the roof of a massive cavern that was open on one side. The water plummeted down for three hundred yards before crashing into a pool surrounded by trees. We snapped our wings open and flew free of the spray, gliding into a cavern so full of lush greenery that we could barely see the rocky walls. We flew over treetops and scared up a flock of bright red parrots before we settled onto a sandy little beach. The river was again wide and slow, flowing lazily out of the cavern.

"Evelyn gazed back at the waterfall, then eyed me. Her smile was a flash of white teeth. 'That was amazing!' She twined her fingers in mine—a physical touch that we rarely shared. I lived for that smile, that pure acceptance of me as just ... me. And for a short time, I was truly happy."

I tried to say 'The End' but the words caught in my throat. A lie. The story hadn't ended there, but I didn't have the heart to tell the next bit. I scratched the back of my neck and glanced at Inez, trying to think of a truthful ending.

Inez cleared her throat and Beatrix jumped, surprised to find her mother listening in. Inez nodded toward the stairs. "Daddy has breakfast ready for you. Say thank you for the story."

"Thank you!" Beatrix beamed and scrambled off the bed to thunder downstairs.

Inez looked at me, concern in her eyes. "You said 'happy for a time.' What happened?"

My fists tightened on the covers, but I met her immortal gaze. "That was the day that Cain murdered Abel, inspired by *my* ill-considered words just before I left with Evelyn. I'd gone gallivanting off like a love-struck schoolboy, and the world changed while I was gone. I'd hoped to find eternal happiness. Instead, I barely avoided Judgment and became the Grim Reaper. Losing my wings was a small price to pay. Losing Evelyn, however..." I trailed off, and Inez nodded.

"Well, there's breakfast when you're ready. Take your time." She left, gently closing the door.

I sat slumped against the wall for several long moments. That day with Evelyn had been marvelous. A truly happy memory of a time when I would have done anything for Evelyn's smile.

I missed that smile. The way her world lit up when she saw me. Evelyn hated me now. Rightfully so, I'd condemned her to an eternity in Abaddon. Yet somehow, she'd escaped.

Would she agree to help me kill the Auditor? We'd been happy once, though that was so long ago. Perhaps I could remind her of our time together. Would remembered joy overcome a lifetime of pain?

I hoped so. It was a small hope, but the only one I had. I no longer hoped to find Evelyn's smile.

Chapter 21

A Pancake, A Suit, and A Cat

Morning ablutions remained a mystery to me, but I once again showered (I survived), defecated (my dignity did *not* survive), and dressed in the one suit I had. The brown tweed was blood-stained and starting to itch. It needed cleaning, but I didn't have any other clothing options.

I contemplated shaving off Frank's beard. There was a razor in the guest bathroom, but the thought of placing a blade to my throat made me shudder. I'd already survived the shower and the defecation. Best not to press my luck.

Feeling marginally ready to face the day, I strolled downstairs.

Breakfast was waiting, the coffee smelled fresh, and the table was a disaster.

I sat down opposite Beatrix. Syrup and bits of pancake spread from her plate in concentric circles. Like rubble after a bomb explodes. She had a fork in one hand, a butter knife in the other, and her tongue between her teeth as she struggled to cut her pancake.

Sam leaned forward from the head of the table. "Let me help, sweetie."

"No!" Beatrix pulled her silverware away, half-sliding the pancake onto the wooden tabletop. Syrup oozed off her plate, joining previously freed puddles.

Sam's lips pursed and Inez, who sat on Beatrix's other side, said, "She won't learn if you always do things for her." Inez used her silverware to help Beatrix retrieve her pancake—sans half its syrup—and said to her daughter, "Here, like this." She cut a slice of her own pancake. "Try again."

Beatrix's tongue resumed its position between her teeth, and she carefully cut a slice. It was too big for a single bite, but she forked it up and shoved it into her mouth, smearing syrup around her lips.

I shuddered and served myself pancakes, eggs, and coffee. My stomach rumbled, so I dove in. Once I'd downed a few bites, I turned to Sam. "I need your help with something."

His eyebrows rose politely. "What's that?"

"I need to talk to Evelyn, but I can't go back to the Land of Evil Auditors."

"Because that demon's looking for you?"

"Xandu. Yes."

"Odd name for a demon. Isn't that another name for paradise?"

"That's Xanadu, which wasn't a paradise. It was just a beautiful city with a dark history which doesn't exist anymore. Xandu is much older and much more evil."

"Huh. You want me to banish him for you?"

My gaze turned to Beatrix. Sam smiled.

"Eh, don't worry about her. I tell Beatrix all about banishing demons. Makes for entertaining bedtime stories."

Beatrix nodded gravely and shoved the last bite of pancake into her mouth. Then she said something that sounded like, "Daddy fights bawakassy," but I couldn't be sure.

"Don't talk with your mouth full," Sam said, "and yes, I fight bureaucracy in all its forms. Be they administrative or demonic."

Inez rose and gathered her plate and Beatrix's. "Alright young lady, time to clean up! Daddy needs to get to work, and you look like you bathed in syrup."

A pout settled onto Beatrix's face, and she stopped chewing, cheeks puffed out like a chipmunk. Inez seemed unfazed and ushered her daughter out of the dining room.

Sam sipped his coffee and asked again, "So, you want me to banish that demon, Xandu?"

I shook my head. "It's not so simple as that. Xandu isn't just a bureaucrat, though he works for the Auditor. He's a warrior. If you went up against him, chances are high that *you* would be one whose soul ended up in Hell."

Sam shrugged, unconvinced. "So, what do you need?"

"I need you to invite the new intern Elizabeth over for dinner tonight so that Evelyn comes with her."

Sam's eyes narrowed, and he nibbled on some bacon. He pointed the bacon at me. "And?"

"I need Evelyn's help."

"You mentioned. Doing what?"

"Solving my Auditor problem."

"How?"

"What's with the twenty questions?"

Sam smiled. "Just seeing what I'm getting myself into."

I sighed. "If Evelyn can take the Auditor out of the picture, I can focus on reversing Frank's spell without constantly looking over my shoulder."

"And how exactly would she 'take the Auditor out of the picture?'"

I leaned forward and lowered my voice. Beatrix and Inez were in the kitchen rinsing dishes, and I didn't want the little girl to overhear. "Evelyn has *Mercy*. I need her to kill the Auditor."

Sam's brows shot up, and he lowered his voice to match. "I thought you didn't kill people. That Death only reaped their souls."

"Desperate times call for desperate measures."

"Something tells me that killing a senior demon would have ... repercussions."

"Less than letting him take over as the Reaper himself. Heaven, Hell, and Earth aren't ready for that!"

"You make him sound worse than the Devil." Sam's fingers tapped at his coffee mug, and he eyed me.

"Let me put it this way: Lucifer is evil, but the kind

of evil that humans revel in. He understands human nature and panders to your vices. The Auditor, on the other hand, believes in a more systemic form of evil. He may not have invented bureaucracy, but he certainly perfected it. To him, humans are no more than numbers on a cosmic balance sheet—a balance sheet that he believes should result in *all* souls going to Hell. The realms are *not* ready for the Auditor to become the Reaper."

Sam whistled and sat back, looking thoughtful. I continued.

"The Auditor is head of the Office of Micromanagement. Eliminate him, and Hell itself will grind to a halt as bloody-minded bureaucratic demons vie for dominance. *That* would give me the time I need to find Frank and reverse his spell. And, as a side benefit for you, Hell's bureaucratic interference in the mortal realm would taper off precipitously. For a time, at least. Until some new fiend assumed control of Micromanagement."

Water splashed in the kitchen. Beatrix seemed to be getting more on the floor than her plate, but Inez remained patient. Sam frowned for several seconds before he nodded.

"All right. I'm not saying I agree with your plan, but I'll

figure out how to get Elizabeth and Evelyn here for dinner. Having another ally couldn't hurt, regardless of whether she agrees to help you or not."

"Thank you." A thought dawned on me, and I dug into my pocket for Frank's keys. "One other favor. Could you stop by Frank's house on your way home? He has a cat named Diana who will be hungry."

I hadn't seen Diana since I'd asked her to go to Abigail in Torments. I didn't know whether she'd actually gone visiting or not, but she would be hungry by now. I jangled Frank's keys toward Sam, hopeful.

He arched an eyebrow. "I don't like cats."

"It's not like I can go," I said. "The Auditor has Xandu hunting me. That's the whole reason I abandoned Frank's life."

Sam sighed and took the keys. "Anything else?"

I decided to ignore the sarcasm in his voice. "I could use some clean clothes."

Sam rolled his eyes. "I shouldn't have asked. I really don't want to go through Frank's underwear drawer."

"Might I remind you that *you* stabbed *me*." I pointed toward the bloodstain on my suit jacket.

Sam held up his hands in surrender and took the keys.

"Fine. I'll see what I can do."

"Something black, if you can find it." I needed to look my best at dinner tonight. Not that a clean suit would convince Evelyn to help me, but my current wardrobe screamed 'desperate fugitive,' which wasn't the impression I wanted to give.

I needed to look more like myself. More like Death.

A black suit wasn't the same as my cowl, but I could settle for being a well-dressed Frank-shaped version of Death. For now.

Chapter 22

THE REAPING OF GARRICK THORSSON

AFTER LUNCH, BEATRIX WENT to preschool, and Inez invited me to join her at work. Interested to see what an immortal did with her time—even if she didn't know she was an immortal—I agreed.

The Grand Estates seemed a rather presumptuous name for the sprawling assisted living facility. It was a brick-faced single-story building that took up an entire block and looked more like a cheap hotel than any sort of grand estate I'd visited.

And I've visited them all. Death comes for rich and poor alike.

The interior was just as unassuming. Wide hallways with tan-painted walls, stark florescent lights, and worn blue carpets that appeared to have a repeating paisley design. If you looked really closely.

The competing sounds of too many televisions cranked to full volume drifted from the apartments, many of whose doors lay wide open.

Inez brought me into an office to the right of the entrance. She introduced me to her coworkers as a friend from out of town who would be joining her on her rounds. The other nurses, mostly middle-aged women, seemed unconcerned with my presence. I received a couple of polite nods.

Inez's boss, however, was a different matter. Marylyn Weaver—sixty-four years old, death in twelve years—was a stout black woman with a severe gray bun and the ingrained wrinkles around her eyes that one gets from a lifetime of scowling. Her breath smelled strongly of nicotine barely covered by the spearmint gum she masticated like a cow. She eyed me with such disapproval that I checked to ensure I hadn't missed a button or spilled coffee on my suit.

No, I still looked like Frank. Flabby, cheap, and scruffy. There was that bloodstain on my suit's right shoulder, but she'd barely glanced at that. Perhaps I should have shaved.

Marylyn cleared her throat and scowled at Inez.

"Your friend will have to leave. I don't need a stranger bumbling around causing problems."

Inez crossed her arms. "Grim also works in end-of-life care, he won't get in the way."

Marylyn cocked an eyebrow at me. "Yeah? What's your field?"

"I care for their souls."

Marylyn blanched, and her eyes bulged. She crossed herself. "Oh, Father, I'm so sorry. I meant no offense. Why didn't you say you were a priest?"

Because I'm not. "No offense taken."

"I have to say, Grim is an odd name for a priest. Although, I guess I've heard odder. There was a priest named Time at the catholic school I attended, and we girls always giggled when Father Time came around. It didn't help that he looked the death warmed over. All skin and bone he was."

I smiled, the name triggering a memory. Father Time

had been a cheerful sort. We'd shared a laugh after I'd said, 'Father Time, your time has come.'

Inez grabbed a clipboard and said, "We really should start my rounds. Anything happen yesterday I should be aware of?"

Marylyn's expression resumed its customary scowl. "Garrick Thorsson in 103 slipped into a coma yesterday. We thought he'd passed, but he's hanging on. Barely."

"Oh, dear. Poor Garrick." Inez glanced at me, but I remained silent. I assumed this was another undeath, like at Wehling Memorial. Without a proper Grim Reaper who was doing his job—damn it, Frank!—Garrick Thorsson would remain in limbo, his body wasting away while his soul remained aware.

A cloud passed over Marylyn's face, and she turned toward me. "Father Grim, I'd appreciate it if you'd look in on him. Garrick has no remaining family."

"Of course," I said with a polite nod.

Clipboard in hand, Inez took my arm and led me down the hallway. We stepped into Room 103 to find a desiccated husk laying upon the bed. Garrick Thorsson wore a nondescript gray sweatshirt, and a purple and green patchwork quilt was drawn up to his chest. The tiny apartment was packed with the summary of Garrick's life: family pictures, memorabilia, and cheap trinkets. Garrick's sallow body had the look and smell of death, but intermittent raspy breaths caught my ear. Medical monitors kept silent vigil by his side.

I stepped to Garrick's bedside and pulled back an eyelid to gaze into his soul. My jaw clenched. As I suspected, he should have moved on yesterday. His body tried to die between each raspy breath, but his lingering soul wouldn't let it.

Frank's cell phone rang, and I wrenched it from my pocket.

"What?"

That infernal mechanical voice greeted me, yet again. "Hi, I've been trying to reach you about your car's extended warranty."

"Go away!"

"Our records indicate that—"

My teeth ground. "I don't want a damned extended warranty!" I glanced at Inez, who gave a knowing eye roll.

"—your Honda Accord's warranty is about to exp—"

The voice cut off abruptly with a series of clicks. Abigail came on the line and spoke in a rush of words.

"Grim, are you there?"

"Abigail?" Relief flooded through me. "How are you?"

There was a brief pause before she said, "Surprisingly good, all things considered. I made a new friend yesterday."

"A fluffy white cat named Diana?"

Abigail inhaled sharply. "How did you know?"

"We're, uh, roommates. Or we were until yesterday."

"Hmmm." I could hear the smile in Abigail's voice, but then her tone became serious. "I'm calling because I found Alvin. I don't know where he's been, but he just stormed into his office. Shall I connect you?"

"Please!"

There was another series of clicks followed by Alvin's nasal voice. "I said no calls!"

"Alvin, it's Grim."

Silence stretched for a moment. "Boy, you have some nerve."

"What?"

"You ambushed me!"

"I did nothing of the sort!"

"Bullshit. Not only were you having coffee with Sam—who's banished me once already—but then your old girlfriend shows up? With *Mercy?* Yeah, I recognized her sword. She almost killed me! Not banished, Grim … *killed!*" Alvin's voice turned shrill with remembered panic.

I drew a deep breath and motioned for Inez to close Garrick's apartment door. "I didn't know she'd attack you, Alvin. I'm sorry. I was as surprised as you were to see Evelyn yesterday."

"Oh, that makes me feel *sooo* much better! You owe me big time for this one!"

My grip tightened around the phone. "Oh, how quickly you forget, Alvin Bureaucracy. *You* owe *me!* Or have you forgotten who gave Frank his soul-swapping spell in a fit of pique? Give me the reversal, and we'll call it even."

Alvin cleared his throat, anger abruptly replaced with something that sounded suspiciously like chagrin. "Yeah, uh, about that. The thing is—"

"Do you have the reversal? Yes or no."

"Uh, no. Unless you can convince Frank to share a cup of Sumerian-priest-bone tea again, there's no swapping back. Sorry, Grim, you're stuck as a human."

My last thread of hope snapped, and I collapsed into Garrick's recliner like a marionette whose strings were cut.

A massive lump seized my throat, stealing my response. Inez laid a concerned hand on my shoulder. I glanced up.

"How...?" Words failed me.

Abigail cut in. I hadn't realized that she'd stayed on the line. "I'm sorry, Grim. Is there anything else you can do? Any way we can help you from here?"

I shook my head, realized that she couldn't see me, and said, "I ... I don't know." That damned lump stopped my words again. I swallowed.

Alvin cleared his throat. "Uh, Grim? I hate to be the bearer of more bad news, but..."

"What?" What could be worse than the news he'd just given?

"Hell's Resources have noticed your absence. The regular flow of souls has dropped to a trickle. They have the Auditor and the Office of Micromanagement looking into it." The Auditor ran the Office of Micromanagement.

"I'm aware," I said. "I saw Xandu yesterday at Frank's office looking for him. For me."

"Yeah, Micromanagement is putting a full-court press on this."

And this was why I needed Evelyn's help. Kill the Auditor and hamstring the Office of Micromanagement so I could track down Frank and solve my mortality problem.

"But that's not the worst part," Alvin continued. "They've taken soul-retrieval into their own claws—"

My head snapped up. "Wait, what?"

"—and they're bypassing Purgatory and Judgment. The Auditor's demons are dragging souls straight to Hell."

I shot to my feet. "But that's against the Rules!"

"Grim, please." Alvin's verbal eye roll was clear. "This is the Office of Micromanagement we're talking about. They must have found some loophole created by your absence."

I swore. Motion at the door made me turn, and I froze. Inez followed my gaze, but I knew she saw nothing.

Xandu slid through the solid door, twin scimitars crossed on his back, beady red eyes fixed on the clipboard in his clawed hand. Muscles bulged under his tight suit as he made a checkmark with a cheap ballpoint. When he spoke, his voice rumbled like a bear's growl.

"Garrick Thorsson, your time is past." Xandu strode to the near-corpse and glanced at Inez and me as he passed.

I averted my eyes; I couldn't let him read my soul. Had he recognized me? Had he seen me recognize him?

Xandu's eyebrows rose, and a sharp-toothed grin pulled

at his scars. He chuckled deeply and made another check-mark.

"Two for one. I knew you were here somewhere, Frank Totmann."

How? How had he tracked me down?

As if in answer, Xandu waggled an imperious claw. "Those extended warranty bots in Customer Annoyance are surprisingly accurate at pinpointing locations."

The ... *what?*

I pulled the phone away from my ear and stared at it. *Idiot!* I'd abandoned Frank's life but kept his phone. And then, like the fool I was, I'd answered every time that Hell called.

I dropped the phone onto the recliner while Xandu turned his focus on Garrick. I grabbed Inez's elbow and whispered sharply, "We need to leave. Now."

Confusion pinched her eyebrows. She glanced from the door to me to Garrick. "What—"

Garrick screamed, and we both jumped. We spun toward the bed. Xandu leaned over Garrick, the claws of his left hand deep in the man's chest. The scream rose in pitch, making the hair on my neck stand on end, and Garrick flailed under the covers as if seeking a lifeline. Xandu pulled upward and Garrick's body arched like a bow until only his head and heels touched the bed. Garrick's scream warbled until, with a jerk, the demon yanked his soul free.

The body collapsed, finally dead.

Inez wrenched her arm from my grip and rushed to the bed, unaware that she was stepping through Xandu's and Garrick's souls.

Garrick hung limply in Xandu's grip. He no longer wore the non-descript sweatshirt, but denim overalls and a red plaid shirt. He looked thirty years younger with fuller cheeks and more hair. The soul takes the form of one's own mental image, so this was how Garrick pictured himself. Despite his soul's healthy tone, Garrick stared blankly into space; shock etched his features.

Fury twisted my gut, and I snarled. That reaping was an abomination! Departed souls should be handled with care, not torn from their bodies!

Xandu turned, chuckling with evil delight. "And now for you, Frank Totmann." He tucked his clipboard under his left arm, which held Garrick, and reached toward me with his clawed right hand.

My fury curdled into fear so fast that my feet seemed to act on their own. I had no defense. Nothing to stop Xandu from wrenching my soul free as well.

Cold dread settled in my stomach. I turned and ran.

Chapter 23

A DEAD END

GARRICK'S APARTMENT DOOR ONLY gave me a moment's resistance. I was learning the tricks inherent in different handles and this one was a simple lever.

I thundered into the hall and bowled right into Marylyn and a bevy of nurses. Garrick's violent demise must have brought them running. Marylyn collapsed in a heap, and I landed atop her. The head nurse's breath whooshed out in a gush of spearmint-laced nicotine that made me blanch.

"Get off of me!" she wheezed and pushed on my chest. I rolled aside and scrambled to my feet, fumbling in my haste. The nurses flowed out of my way, and I stumbled into the wall. A nurse helped Marylyn stand while the others peered into Garrick's room.

Marylyn grabbed my lapel and pointed through the door toward Garrick's corpse—and inadvertently pointed directly at Xandu who was eying me with a bemused expression.

"What did you do?" Marylyn snarled.

I opened my mouth, closed it, opened it again like an idiot, then grimaced. I *really* needed to learn how to compose myself in a crisis. Gaping like a bloody dying fish was embarrassing! But what could I say? How could I explain what had just happened without sounding crazy?

Xandu strolled unhurriedly through the open door, dragging a limp and ephemeral Garrick by the front of his overalls. The deceased's soul shook his head, seeming to come to his senses.

Hold on. Marylyn thought I was a priest. I could tell the truth, and she'd accept it at face value.

"Demon," I said, pointing at Xandu standing in the doorway. Two of the nurses said, "What?" simultaneously while Marylyn arched an eyebrow.

Xandu's expression, however, was one of confirmed suspicions. He glanced at Marylyn, as if to verify that she couldn't see him and nodded at her confused scowl.

He was invisible to all but me.

"Well, well," Xandu said. "You *can* see me. That will make this *much* more fun." A chilling smile pulled at his scars.

I still had no plan. Time to run.

I knocked Marylyn's hand from my lapel and bolted between two nurses. There were yells for me to stop, to come back, but I ignored them. The hallway turned right, and I skidded around the corner.

A granny with a walker blocked my path. I dodged left, bounced off the wall, and shouted, "Sorry!" as I slid past. I glanced back, doing an awkward sideways stumble as I tried to maintain speed.

Xandu was only yards behind me, keeping pace without effort. He passed through the granny without pausing, and she stopped, a shiver wracking her frail body. Lung-deep coughs made her clutch her walker.

Garrick, for his part, had fully come around. He struggled in Xandu's iron grip and pried at the demon's fist which was closed around the bib of his overalls. "Leggo me, ya ugly goat!"

"Silence, worm!" Xandu shook Garrick.

"Help! Help! I've been kidnapped by a demon!"

Xandu slowed his implacable pace long enough to lift Garrick's soul to eye level and sneer. "Your soul belongs to Hell! Be silent while I collect *his* soul"—Xandu pointed at me—"or the pain of your death will pale beside the torments to come!"

Garrick bit Xandu's left forearm.

"Ow! Stop that!" Xandu shook Garrick again, but the wiry old man bared down and shook his head like a terrier with a bone. "Ow!"

Reaching another corner, I turned right and lost sight of my pursuer. This hallway curved further to the right past more apartment doors, many of which were open. Most of the residents didn't even notice my frantic scramble over their blaring televisions.

"Lemme go! Lemme go, you varmint!" Garrick's voice echoed down the hall. Xandu was close. I tried to put on a burst of speed, to sprint, but I had no more to give.

Frank's body wasn't built for exercise. I'd been running full tilt for under two minutes and already stars flared at the edges of my vision. My breath was heavy and labored, and my heart pounded on my ribs like a prisoner desperate for escape.

I'd already had two heart attacks this week. I couldn't afford another. Not now.

I slowed at the end of the curved hall. It was a T-junction. I turned left for no better reason than that I'd turned right the last time.

Dead end. Damn!

There was a door with a crash bar like I'd used at the Land of Evil Auditors. I slammed bodily into it.

It didn't open.

I bounced hard from the locked door and fell back, collapsing heavily to the floor. I sucked in deep breaths and tried to stand. My legs felt watery from my mad sprint, but I made it to my knees before I felt Xandu's presence behind me. I turned.

The demon tried to loom, but his ability to intimidate by pure presence was tarnished by Garrick, who refused to go quietly into the night. The wiry old man had wrapped himself around Xandu's left arm and was biting, scratching, and screaming at him.

"I ain't goin' to Hell!" Bite, scratch. "I'm a son of Thor who's going down fightin'!" Punch, kick. "I'm going to Valhalla!"

Xandu clenched his jaw and glared down at me, clearly

trying to ignore Garrick Thorsson. "Frank Totmann, you can't run from Death."

I snarled, sucking in labored breaths. "You are *not* Death. You're nothing more than a messenger with delusions of grandeur." I struggled to my feet, shoulders back, fists clenched. I'd be damned if I met my end on my knees.

Xandu's eyes narrowed. He tried to meet my gaze, but I didn't let him. It was bad enough that he thought I was Frank Totmann. Heaven help me if he found out who I *really* was. Xandu shrugged, making his skin-tight suit ripple. "The time for running and bluster is over!" His bear-like growl burned with confidence.

My back hit the locked door. I was trapped. I couldn't fight, I couldn't run.

Garrick punched Xandu in the left temple, just below his horn.

The demon's head rocked aside then whipped back with a snarl. He roared like an enraged beast and shook the old man's soul.

Garrick grinned. Then he kicked Xandu in the stomach, turning the roar into a grunt.

Realization hit me like a freight train, stealing my labored breath. My jaw dropped before I clicked it shut.

I couldn't fight Xandu … but Garrick could.

The old man could save us both.

"Garrick!" I yelled, and his head whipped around. "Take his scimitar!" I pointed at the handle poking over Xandu's left shoulder.

Both Garrick and Xandu glanced at the scimitar. There was a pause—a joint moment of dawning comprehension—before they both reached for the infernal blade.

Garrick was faster.

He whipped the scimitar free and swung it at Xandu's neck.

Xandu ducked, the blade nicked his horn, and he dropped to one knee.

The deceased soul landed on his feet and chopped downward at the arm still clutching his overalls. It was an awkward attack, and I doubted Garrick was a practiced swordsman. Regardless, the blade bit deeply into Xandu's left arm, just below the elbow.

No blood sprang forth—demons don't bleed—but a gaseous black substance drifted upward like curling cigar smoke. Xandu's red eyes bulged. He screamed, a banshee howl of pain.

Garrick slammed his free palm on the back of the scimitar's blade, and it chopped clean through. He stumbled back, Xandu's clawed hand still attached to his overalls.

Xandu's scream cut off, and he stared at his severed limb in shock. I suspected this was the first time that a human soul had bested him. I hoped it wouldn't be the last.

"Ha!" Garrick crowed, leaping away from Xandu and waving the blade at him. "That'll teach you to steal good men's souls! Hell ain't taking me. Not now, not ever!" The old man capered, waving the sword around. He wrenched the severed hand from his overalls and flung it at Xandu. It bounced off the demon's chest, then wafted into the ether like inky smoke.

I sagged in relief. He'd done it!

Free from Xandu's grip, Garrick's soul could now disappear into the ether and head to Purgatory to await Judgment. I doubted that he'd be headed toward damnation.

Garrick did not disappear.

He glanced at me, threw a cocky salute, and dashed through the nearest wall, scimitar in hand.

I realized what I'd just done, and my lips pursed.

I'd created a ghost.

It wasn't the end of the world—that wasn't due for at least another millennium—but ghosts were notoriously difficult to track down.

But that was a problem for another day. Right now, I needed to escape. Could I run past Xandu without him grabbing me?

Perhaps. His gaze was still locked on the inky smoke wafting from his shortened arm.

Now or never. I braced myself against the locked door and prepared to run.

Chapter 24

MIRACLES THROUGH EMPOWERMENT

THE DOOR BEHIND ME popped open, and I fell backward into someone's arms. Inez.

What? How...?

"Come on," she whispered, glancing at the hallway. She couldn't see the wounded Xandu, and he didn't see her. His shocked gaze was firmly fixed on the stump of his left arm. Inez pulled me through the doorway and eased it shut.

We were in a wide utility and storage room. Shelves of

cleaning supplies sat opposite a furnace and water heater. Inez took my hand and led me at a jog to an open door on the far side. Her minivan sat just outside, doors open, engine running.

I leapt into the back, she into the driver's seat, and Inez tore out of the parking lot before I even figured out how to close the sliding door.

"How—"

My question was cut off when Inez turned onto the road at speed, and I tumbled across the bench seat. I caught my breath, braced myself behind the passenger seat, and started again. "How did you know where I was?"

She grinned at me in the rearview mirror. "The Grand Estates isn't that big. You ran toward the utility room. It wasn't that hard to figure out."

"Thank you. Your timing was impeccable." I braced myself as we rounded another corner.

"Any demons chasing us?" she asked.

I glanced back but saw no sign of Xandu. "No, we're clear."

Inez slowed, turned onto a major thoroughfare, and merged with the mid-afternoon traffic.

My brows furrowed. "You are surprisingly adept at escape and evasion."

Her eyes twinkled in the mirror. "What, you think this was my first time escaping the forces of Hell? My husband *is* a demon hunter. It comes with the territory."

"How exactly *did* Sam get into demon hunting?" He had been cagey about the details, perhaps Inez would be more talkative.

She threw an apologetic smile over her shoulder. "Sorry, that's Sam's story to tell, not mine. You'll have to ask him."

Blast. I held my tongue, but curiosity burned inside me. Who were the Davidsons? A demon hunter and an immortal who I'm pretty sure was unaware of her uniqueness. There had to be one hell of a story there.

I was impressed with Inez's courage, though. She couldn't see the forces arrayed against her, yet still she fought by her husband's side. And seemingly without fear.

Perhaps that was the key to unraveling the mystery of Inez's pending immortality. Something was going to happen during their fight against Hell that would somehow preclude her death.

What that might be, I had no idea.

Inez's phone rang, and she answered it. I heard Marylyn's voice yelling through the phone. Inez apologized profusely for bringing me in, promised that I'd never return to The Grand Estates again, then asked if she could have the remainder of the day off to deal with her troublesome houseguest.

I might have taken offense at the comment, but she winked at me as she said it.

How touching, Inez was lying to Marylyn on my behalf. But was it a lie? I *was* her houseguest and had certainly caused trouble. Perhaps it was the truth, but the words felt deceitful. A shaded truth perhaps.

I watched the passing city as Inez dickered with Marylyn about swapping shifts. Tightly packed houses on my right, single-story businesses on my left. Pawn shops, lawyers, and pay-day loans blended into a crumbling miasma of brick-faced avarice, broken only by the occasional gas station and fast-food restaurant. The houses on the right dropped away behind us to reveal a large park with brown grass and a metal playground that had seen better days.

I abruptly realized that I was enjoying the drive. Or, at least, I wasn't quivering in terror, which I supposed wasn't quite the same thing. Inez was much less dramatic in her driving habits than Louis.

Inez's scowl said that negotiations weren't going well,

but eventually she said thank you and hung up.

I cleared my throat. "I'm sorry I got you in trouble at work."

Inez shook the scowl from her face. "Don't worry about it. It's not the first time a demon has screwed up my life. It won't be the last. At least I didn't get fired this time."

I nodded and eyed the city. The ridgeline was behind us, but other than that I didn't recognize anything. "Where are we going?"

"Grocery shopping."

I raised an eyebrow. "Do you normally go grocery shopping after fleeing the forces of Hell?" Was this some coping mechanism? I'd assumed we would return to the Davidson's home to hunker down. Hide.

Inez raised a matching eyebrow. "I'm hosting a young lady and her guardian angel for dinner tonight. I'm not serving leftovers."

Ah, so Inez was merely being practical. Excellent. "What did you have in mind?"

"Kale and chicken salad."

"Hmmm. I've never had kale. Is it any good?" Memories of the cold chicken from Frank's fridge made my mouth water. My stomach made annoying little gurgling noises, despite having lunch not long ago.

Alvin had been right. The amount of food the human body required was simply ridiculous.

Inez smiled and turned into a half-full grocery store parking lot. "Kale's a staple at our house. Sam's not a huge fan, but he can complain once he starts cooking."

Several minutes later, I found myself pushing a cart down the massive store's bewildering aisles. Inez led the way, occasionally stopping to pluck something from a shelf and drop it into the cart.

I eyed the shelves. How the hell did Inez determine what she wanted? The available selections were staggering! I counted over twenty different options for sugar alone. I didn't have time to count the types of coffee, we weren't in that aisle long enough.

So many decisions.

Inez pulled a small bag from amongst a dozen other small bags and tossed it into the cart. Dried cranberries.

"So," she said over her shoulder, "Alvin couldn't find the reversal for your, um, condition. What will you do now?"

I sighed and leaned heavily on the cart as we paused again. Chopped walnuts joined the dried cranberries. "I don't know."

"Okay, let's break the problem down. What do you need above all else?" We turned into an aisle dedicated entirely to cheese. My nose twitched, and my stomach grumbled.

I pursed my lips. "I need to find Frank."

"How hard could that be? He found you."

"Yes, by timing his death."

"So, you die and wait for Frank to reap your soul."

"I doubt he'd even show up. Remember the Coma Conundrum on the news? The undead bodies I saw at Wehling Memorial? Frank's not doing his job. The Auditor's minions are more likely to show up than he is. They'd rip my soul from this body as Xandu did to Garrick Thorsson! No, that's not a chance I can take."

"I still think you should ask Heaven for help. Are you sure Gabriel won't talk to you?" She leaned over the cheese display and thumbed through plastic-wrapped blocks of yellow and white.

I grimaced. After millennia of bad blood, Gabriel was more likely to execute the long-delayed Judgment for my original sin and replace me than to help. Was that a chance I could take?

"Perhaps he would," I said. "But I'm not crossing that bridge until after I've dealt with the Auditor."

Inez pointed a small block of blue-marbled cheese at me. A rancid odor made me jerk back, and she grinned. "No, not after. Now. Today." Inez dropped the cheese into the cart and headed toward the front of the store.

I hurried to catch up, weaving around other shoppers. "It's not that simple!"

"Sure it is," she called over her shoulder. "How do you contact Heaven?"

"I don't, and that's the problem. Heaven doesn't like talking to me, so I'm generally happy to return the favor."

"Hmmm..." She reached a register and began unloading the cart onto the small conveyor belt. "Do prayers work?"

I frowned. "For the faithful, yes. Though the answers often aren't what they want to hear. The Almighty's preferred responses seem to be, 'No,' or 'Not right now, I'm busy,' which might explain the general decline in faith-based miracles over the past two millennia."

The cashier, a young man with a nose ring and dreadlocks pulled back into a ponytail, raised his eyebrows as he scanned the groceries, but refrained from comment.

Inez grabbed the first full bag and returned it to the cart. "But prayers *do* reach Heaven."

I nodded reluctantly.

The cashier cleared his throat, glanced between us, and told Inez the price. She dutifully paid with her credit card. She waved me forward, so I pushed the cart toward the exit. As we stepped outside, a brisk wind plucked at my suit jacket and pushed Inez's short red hair across her face.

"So," she continued, pushing her hair behind an ear, "we just need to find someone whose prayers do reach heaven and have them pass a message for you."

"What? No!" I stopped short of her minivan. "Prayer isn't asking *Gabriel* for help. That's going straight to the top! I can't ask the Almighty to intervene."

"Why not?"

"It's not like He'd help."

"Again, why not?" Inez grabbed the front of the cart, pulled it the rest of the way to her minivan, and started unloading. I crossed my arms.

"Refer back to my previous comment about the current state of divine answers. 'No' or 'Not right now.' Besides, the Almighty usually prefers people find their own solutions. Miracles through empowerment, I think He calls it."

Inez eyed me sideways, and then pushed the cart to join its mates in a little cart corral. We climbed into the minivan—I joined her up front this time—and she started the engine. She paused with her hand on the gearshift and turned toward me. "I would have thought that a spirit who *knows* that Heaven and Hell are real would have a little more faith."

"The Almighty is an enigma, even to the angels who serve Him. To claim to understand Him and His Plan is pure foolishness."

"You don't think that reinstating you as the Grim Reaper falls within His Plan?"

I drummed my fingers on the door armrest. "I don't know. What if there is no Plan and we're all just bumbling around like dice in a cosmic game of chance? It's the not knowing that scares me."

Inez snorted and threw the minivan into gear. "Welcome to being human. We never know what's going to happen. Whether outcomes are part of some divine Plan or fate, or pure random chance doesn't matter. Crippling indecision is a recipe for failure. Make your own plans and act. We'll deal with the fallout later." She nodded as if that was the end of the discussion and backed out of her parking space.

We drove in silence. Inez toyed absently with the ring

on her right hand, a narrow thing woven of three separate bands of white, yellow, and rose gold. There was wisdom in what Inez said, but I shook my head. "I can't go to the Almighty. It's too risky, but,"—I drew a ragged breath—"I will seek out Gabriel after I've dealt with the Auditor."

Inez opened her mouth to argue, but I held up a forestalling hand. "No, you told me to make a decision, and I've made it. Today's focus is convincing Evelyn to help me."

She pursed her lips but let the argument drop. After a minute of silence, she turned on the radio and started flipping through stations. Talk radio and advertisements for used cars filled the minivan before a familiar voice caught my ear.

"Stop!" I said. "Go back."

Inez tuned the station back to a news broadcast. Damien Nigel's sonorous voice rang from the speakers with a slight crackle.

"—I've spoken with the appropriate authorities about the Coma Conundrum, and we are doing all we can."

Another man with a nasal voice asked, "So what's the plan?"

"We believe that these patients have entered into a new

phase of the dying process." He wasn't wrong. "It's a sad fact, but everybody dies"—correct again—"so the best plan is to care for them as best we can until they pass peacefully."

The interviewer snorted. "Peacefully? Have you *seen* the videos online? Those coma patients died screaming. I wouldn't call that peaceful!"

Videos? What videos? I shared a concerned look with Inez. Nigel's response was smoothly cool.

"I am aware. As with any new process, we are learning as we go, but rest assured that the appropriate authorities are doing all they can to set things right."

My jaw clenched. Set things right? Hell and the Office of Micromanagement were more interested in upping their numbers than in setting things *right*. More souls were suffering as Garrick had. I'd saved him—well, he'd saved himself—but how many more souls would be dragged to Hell in my absence?

I had to stop the Office of Micromanagement, and the only way to do that was to stop the Auditor.

Permanently.

Chapter 25

FULL BATTLE MODE

Upon returning home, Inez immediately went into what she referred to as 'full battle mode.' I expected that to involve collecting weaponry and fortifying defenses. The immortal's true nature was about to come out!

Or not.

Apparently 'full battle mode' was a euphemism for 'the dubious joys of house cleaning.'

After the catastrophe with Xandu and Garrick's soul, I wanted to go into 'full research mode' and learn more about what was happening in the world. Watch those videos that the news had mentioned. But Inez was adamant. An immortal force to be reckoned with. She would *not* be the hostess remembered for scattered toys and messy counters.

Inez called me to a utility room on the far side of the kitchen and thrust a vacuum at me. I eyed the contraption. It looked like a miniature jet engine with a handle. Gray and purple plastic with Model X emblazoned on the side in bold script.

"Ah, a Dyson Model X," I said, remembering my conversation with Louis about his ill-chosen anniversary gift. "Self-propelled, deep cleaning, and light as a feather. Best on the market."

Inez leaned back and eyed me up and down like she'd never seen me before. "The Grim Reaper knows his vacuums! Well, that saves me the trouble of teaching you how to use it."

"I, uh..."

Inez said something about getting Beatrix from the bus stop and slipped past me and out the door.

Blast.

Clearly, Inez had no compunctions against putting her troublesome houseguest to work.

I grumbled and wheeled the contraption to the kitchen.

After ten minutes I unraveled the mystery of how to plug the vacuum in and start it, which pleased me to no end. I was less pleased when it leapt forward like a hellhound straining at its leash. I held on for dear life and hoped it didn't eat anything important.

My ears rang with the noise of the vacuum gobbling up crumbs and lint from the tile. It sounded like someone strangling a racecar engine.

The front door slammed, and Beatrix bolted into the living room. Her small backpack flew onto the couch before bouncing to the floor, dumping its contents. The child slid to a stop in front of a plastic bin on a shelf. Inez called after her, but Beatrix had the bin dumped onto the floor before her mother rounded the corner.

"Oh, no you don't!" Inez yelled over the vacuum. "Snack-time first, *then* you can play." She dragged her recalcitrant child from the living room. As they passed through the kitchen to the dining room, Inez glanced at the vacuum straining to escape my grip. "Thanks for offering to help, Grim. I appreciate it."

I *hadn't* offered, but her gratitude warmed my heart, nonetheless. The Grim Reaper doesn't hear the words 'thank you' very often.

I moved to the living room. I was vacuuming around the mess that had fallen from Beatrix's backpack when her ear-shattering scream made me jump. The Model X leapt from my grip and slammed into the couch. I turned to the hysterical four-year-old who stood behind me. Incoherent screams echoed off the walls, tears streamed down her face, and an accusing finger pointed at the vacuum.

I turned it off, hoping that would resolve the tears.

No. Beatrix continued screaming at a volume usually reserved for the mortally wounded.

Inez rounded the corner from the dining room like a lioness, running at a dead sprint and prepared to eviscerate whoever had harmed her cub. I took a self-preserving step back as Inez's gaze somehow took in the entire scene while remaining focused on her daughter.

"What's wrong, Sweetie?" Her voice was deceptively calm.

Tears. Incoherent screams. Pointing at the hellhound vacuum.

"Did something get vacuumed up?"

Nods. Reduced screaming. Accusing finger now pointed at me.

"Okay." Inez drew a calming breath, and the tension in

her shoulders eased. "Let's see what we can find." She re-moved the vacuum's clear plastic bin, which was half-full of collected dirt and hair. With the care of a surgeon, Inez fished through the detritus and retrieved a crumpled scrap of paper. "Is this what you were looking for?"

Beatrix nodded, her distraught face splotchy. Inez smoothed out the paper and smiled. "Ah, I see." She hand-ed the scrap to Beatrix. "Did you make this at preschool?" The little girl nodded with a sniffle and held it close.

Inez gave me a significant look, then nodded toward her daughter.

I knelt. "I'm terribly sorry. What did I vacuum up?"

Beatrix's lip trembled, but she showed the paper to me. It was small, perhaps the size of my palm, its edges torn roughly into the shape of a tombstone. Scrawled in purple marker was my misspelled name, *Grimm Repr,* bracketed with two little daisies.

"Did you make that for me?"

She nodded.

I extended an open hand. Beatrix handed me the scrap of paper with the solemn intensity of the very young. An odd sensation fluttered through my chest. "Thank you," I said, gently spreading the scrap to reduce its wrinkles. "I will cherish it always."

And I would. It was poorly drawn and with bad spelling, but this little paper tombstone was the most precious gift I'd ever received.

It was the only gift I'd ever received.

With matching solemnity, I folded the paper and slid it into the inner pocket of my suit jacket.

Beatrix leaned into her mother who said, "Alright, kiddo. Let's finish that snack, and then I think someone needs a nap."

Inez and Beatrix returned to the dining room, and I retrieved the paper to gaze at it. A heavy feeling settled on me that I couldn't identify. It wasn't sorrow, exactly, but it felt like it.

Humans are amazing, children doubly so. It's a thankless job, safeguarding their souls, but it's the one thing I'm good at. I am often despised, feared, and ridiculed. Humans can be cruel. But they are also capable of unfathomable kindness. It was a good reminder about why I needed to regain my mantle as Death.

Souls were suffering under Frank's absent care, and not just the elderly. How many children had succumbed to the Coma Conundrum instead of being gently ushered into the afterlife? How many young souls had been ripped from their bodies by demons like Xandu? I shuddered.

Frank had a lot to answer for.

"Death is coming for you, Frank Totmann," I whispered, staring at that little tombstone. I ran a finger along the daisies. "*I* am coming for you."

Chapter 26

UNEXPECTED GUESTS

After the incident with the hellhound vacuum, Inez relieved me of cleaning duties. Something about it being faster to do things herself if she didn't have to watch over my shoulder. But she was kind enough to instruct me on navigating the television remote. Time to go into full research mode.

When Sam returned from the Land of Evil Auditors several hours later, I was sitting on the couch, arms crossed, glowering at the news. Every channel showed the same thing. Unexplained comas followed by violent deaths. I'd caught another interview with Nurse Lisle, but despite her forced smiles for the camera, I recognized the haunted look in her eyes. Her heart was breaking every time she lost a patient.

As did mine.

Inez was in the kitchen preparing the kale and chicken salad for dinner. She didn't glance up from her frying pan when the front door opened, but Beatrix thundered down the stairs yelling, "Daddy!" which was quickly followed by an even more joyous, *"Kitty!"*

I frowned. Sam had brought Diana here? I turned off the television and pushed myself off the couch. In the entryway, I found Sam with a plastic cat carrier in one hand, a cardboard box on the opposite hip, and a tight expression. Thin red scratches graced the backs of both hands.

Diana glared at me from inside the cat carrier and cowered away from Beatrix's questing fingers.

Sam set Diana down and sneezed. "I hate cats."

"You've mentioned," I said. "I didn't expect you to bring her here. Diana seems quite self-sufficient, so long as there's food available."

Sam cocked his head. "You've never had a pet, have you?"

"No. Can you imagine the Grim Reaper showing up

with a puppy? I *do* have a certain image to maintain."

Sam's glower lightened, and one lip quirked into his customary half-smile. "Well, maybe not a puppy. But I could see you with a rat on your shoulder. Especially if you gave him his own cowl and little scythe."

"Ha ha, very funny."

Sam chuckled despite my deadpan. "Anyway, my point is that pets need a lot more care than just leaving out food. Diana's litter looked like it hadn't been cleaned in weeks!"

"Litter? As in trash?" Why would a cat have a trash can?

"No. As in her kitty poop box." He pulled a shallow blue plastic pan from the cardboard box as evidence.

Beatrix burst out laughing. "Kitty poop box!" she said, pointing at it before collapsing to the floor in uncontrolled giggles. Sam rolled his eyes.

I'll admit, I was a bit slow on the uptake. I looked at the blue pan, back to Diana, then at Sam. "Diana's toilet is a plastic bin?"

"Yup. And as her owner, *you're* supposed to clean it. Not me."

Bile climbed up my throat, and I shuddered. "It's bad enough dealing with my own ... defecation. Why on earth would anyone want to clean up after an animal?"

"Wants and needs are two different beasts. If you *want* to have a pet, then you *need* to be prepared to clean up after it."

"I didn't want a pet. I didn't want any of this! I'm just trying to survive this insanity you call life and thought that asking you to look in on Diana was the right thing to do."

Sam ran his fingers through his hair. "Sorry. You're right, Diana's lack of care is Frank's fault, not yours."

Beatrix tugged Sam's pant leg. "Daddy, what's dificas-in?"

He glanced down. "Defecation, sweetie. It's a big word that means poop."

Apparently, scatological humor was a big hit with the four-year-old crowd. Beatrix cackled and scrambled to the kitchen, barely able to talk through her peals of laughter as she tried to share her new word with her mother.

Sam reached down and popped open Diana's cage. The cat hissed at him from the back before shooting out in a fluffy white blur. She darted past me and into the living room to, no doubt, hide under the couch.

"So," I asked Sam once she was gone, "are Elizabeth and Evelyn coming to dinner?"

He nodded. "They are. And, uh, they're not coming

alone. Cora invited herself."

"What?" I liked Cora, she was a good person, but she didn't like *me*. This was not a complication I needed.

Sam waved his hands defensively. "I couldn't think of a logical reason to say no."

I opened my mouth to provide any number of reasons, but no words came out. Besides, it was too late anyway. I was just going to have to deal with Frank's girlfriend—ex-girlfriend?—and hope she didn't get in the way.

"Did you find any fresh clothes?" Considering the state of Frank's house, the availability of clean clothes wasn't a given.

Sam nodded and reached into the box to retrieve a small duffle bag. "A fresh suit—black pinstripe, as requested—socks and other necessities."

I took the bag gratefully and headed upstairs to prepare. I need to look my best. Evelyn was coming to dinner.

Chapter 27

KALE SALAD

CORA AND ELIZABETH—AND EVELYN—ARRIVED within the hour. Evelyn hovered protectively behind the intern's shoulder while Cora swept through the door with her normal clatter of jewelry. Today's matronly dress was green and fuzzy with purple accents, making her look like an overripe plum tree, but one with a warm smile for Sam. Beside her, Elizabeth looked plain and understated in a simple two-tone gray pants suit. They'd clearly come straight from the office.

I watched their entrance from my seat at the dining room table. The dining room sat just to the right of the front door, connected by a wide archway. A smaller archway to my right showed the kitchen, which smelled wonderfully of baked chicken with a lemon and honey glaze. There had been a brief discussion of Beatrix joining us for dinner, but her parents had decided it best to foist her off on the neighbors for the evening.

I nervously fiddled with my fork and watched as Sam and Inez greeted their guests. Butterflies danced a jig in my stomach. I'd initially felt better in the black pinstripe suit—not as imposing as my traditional cloak and cowl, but sharp nonetheless—but my confidence was fading fast. I pressed a hand over the pocket that held Beatrix's tombstone-shaped masterpiece. I could do this. I had to.

Cora caught my gaze, and her cheerful smile dissolved into a scowl. Oh, yes, dinner with her was going to be such a joy!

Evelyn stood with her back to the door, sharp gaze flicking from corner to corner as she scanned for threats. Despite the intensity of her inspection, however, she didn't once look at me. It was as if I had been promoted from active threat to inconsequential furniture.

I wasn't sure that was better.

The fork I was fiddling with slipped from my fingers.

It clattered onto my plate and tried skittering toward the floor. I fumbled, caught it, and set it carefully to the left of my plate where I'd found it. Everyone glanced over at the noise, and Evelyn's hand snapped to *Mercy*'s hilt. When no demons followed the clatter, her grip relaxed. Yet she still didn't look at me.

I drew a calming breath and belatedly realized that I should have joined the greeting committee. I had requested this dinner, and here I sat in silence like a lump on a log.

Well done, Grim. You've started the evening with discourtesy.

Inez disappeared into the kitchen, and Sam led his guests to the table. I pulled my gaze from Evelyn and firmly told the butterflies in my stomach to stop dancing. I rose and extended a hand across the table.

"Good evening, Elizabeth," I said. "How have you found your first two days in the IRS?" Look at that. I didn't sound nervous at all!

"Please, call me Liz."

Right. Humans and their love of shortened names.

Liz shook my hand firmly and sat across from me. I felt that little tingle in my soul again at the empath's touch. Her emotions were positive, but nervous. "Everyone's been much nicer than I expected," she said. "You hear stories about the IRS and, well, let's just say I've been pleasantly surprised."

Sam snorted and claimed his chair at the head of the table, his back to the kitchen. "Give it time. A couple of days isn't enough to truly experience the bureaucratic wasteland of government service."

Cora waved a dismissive hand and sat between Sam and Liz. "Don't listen to him. It's the people who make any workplace enjoyable. Just avoid the duplicitous, and you'll be fine." She fingered the heavy iron cross around her neck and looked pointedly at me.

Duplicitous? I couldn't lie if I tried!

Uncomfortable silence followed Cora's obvious jab.

Thankfully, Inez saved me from defending my honor with a cheerful, "Dinner is served!" as she set a massive salad bowl on the table. She sat between Sam and me. "Please, serve yourselves."

While Cora dished herself, Sam asked Liz where she'd gone to school. I didn't pay attention to her answer.

I was focused on Evelyn, trying to catch her gaze. We couldn't talk in the dining room, there were too many people for what I knew would be an awkward conversation. Especially when half the people didn't even know Evelyn existed.

My lips pursed. It was difficult keeping the dynamics straight of who knew what.

Sam, Inez, and I knew about Evelyn, but only Sam and I could see her. They and Cora knew *my* identity, but Cora didn't know that the Davidsons knew. Did she suspect?

Liz was the only person truly in the dark. If everything worked out as I hoped, she'd remain innocent. Even though Heaven thought her worthy of a guardian angel, few people were prepared to learn the truth about the spiritual war that raged around them.

My eyes narrowed, and I wondered once again: what was so special about Liz that Heaven granted her *Evelyn* as a guardian? Was this a demotion of Evelyn, or was Liz truly that important?

All excellent questions. If only I could get five minutes with Evelyn, I might ask her. I just needed to catch her gaze and get her to follow me to the other room for a quiet chat. So simple.

I cleared my throat.

Evelyn's gaze continued scanning everything but me.

I clenched my jaw. Fine. I'd do this the hard way.

The salad bowl passed to me, and I started dishing. There was a lull in the small talk, and I glanced at Cora. "You were right about needing to avoid certain auditors. Some of them are pure evil. Like the Hell-spawned bureaucrat I ran into today named Xandu." Evelyn's back stiffened, and her hand shifted to *Mercy*'s hilt again. She knew that name.

Liz's eyebrows climbed her forehead. "I haven't met him yet. What's so bad about this Xandu?"

"He likes making others suffer. It's his sole purpose in life."

Cora shook her head. "Who? Is he one of the new hires on the fifth floor?"

"No. I was visiting with a ... client offsite when Xandu showed up." I chose my words with care. I just needed Evelyn's attention. "He tried doing my job for me and made a right mess of it. Inez was there, she can tell you"—and perhaps add some convincing lies for me—"but Xandu basically ripped the man's soul from his body."

That got Evelyn's attention. Her gaze snapped to mine, horror in her dark eyes.

Liz frowned and looked at Inez. "Are you an auditor too?"

Inez shook her head. "No, a nurse."

Liz's frown deepened, and she glanced between us. "And you were with Frank on an audit? Why?"

Inez pursed her lips and eyed me. Okay, so I should have warned her that she might have to lie for me. My bad. While Inez distracted Liz with a tale that sounded half-true, I finally caught Evelyn's gaze. I motioned with my eyes toward the living room.

Evelyn crossed her arms and shook her head.

I nodded more emphatically toward the living room.

Inez cleared her throat. I froze mid-nod. I looked around the table. All eyes were on me. Blast. Had someone asked me a question?

"Um, yes." That seemed like a safe answer. I glanced around the table. Confused expressions said I'd answered wrong. "I meant, no." The confusion deepened. I looked back at Evelyn, who arched an imperious eyebrow.

Liz turned to follow my gaze. She looked back toward me. "Are you okay, Frank? You keep looking over my shoulder."

Cora muttered under her breath, "He most certainly is not okay." Her fingers clutched that Celtic iron cross.

"I'm..." The word 'fine' stuck *again* in my throat.

"It's…" 'Nothing' joined 'fine,' and they danced a little jig around my Adam's apple. Bloody Gabriel and his *bloody* Truth in Death!

Everyone was watching me.

I couldn't lie, but I'd be damned if I told the truth. So, I stabbed a pile of kale salad and stuffed it into my mouth.

Bitterness exploded across my tongue. I tried to swallow, but my throat rebelled. I choked. There was a strangled *hrnk* sound at the back of my throat, and my cheeks puffed out like a chipmunk's.

Inez steepled her fingers and asked with deceptive calm, "So, how's the salad?"

"Bitter as the tears of the damned," I managed, though it was muffled by roughage.

"Oh, come on. Kale's not *that* bitter."

Sam muttered, "Yes, it is," which earned him a scowl. He shoveled in his own mouthful and chewed with an exaggerated look of innocence.

I grabbed my water glass and tried to wash down the kale. It didn't help. The bitterness intensified, and my throat threatened to—

No, I was *not* going to vomit at the dinner table.

Through pure willpower, I chewed, swallowed, and

chased the demon-lettuce with several deep draughts of water.

I drew a shuddering breath and sat back.

Again, everyone was looking at me. Or perhaps they'd never stopped. Inez looked annoyed.

"That was ... an intense flavor," I said.

Sam snorted, and Inez swiveled her glare on him. She brushed her hair behind one ear but said nothing.

Everyone dug into their salads. Liz and Cora seemed to enjoy it and said as much, which made me question their sanity. I fished out bits of chicken with my fork but left the demon-lettuce behind.

Evelyn unfolded her arms and leaned toward me. Her dark eyes bored into mine. "Tell me about Xandu ripping souls free," she said in that gravelly voice that seemed so foreign, yet still familiar. She'd had a clear soprano before Abaddon. What had happened to her in there? "If this is true, Heaven needs to know."

Again, I nodded toward the living room. Evelyn shook her head. "I'm not leaving Elizabeth."

"Oh, come on! I just need five minutes."

Silence fell over the table. Damn! I'd spoken out loud.

Liz again turned to follow my gaze. "Who are you talking to?"

"I … well…"

Sam rolled his eyes and said, "Just tell her."

"But…"

"Did you really expect to keep Liz in the dark?"

I glared at Sam. "I'd hoped to, yes."

Liz folded her arms and sat back. "What's going on here?" Her gaze flicked between us.

Sam gestured to me with a 'go ahead' expression. Liz tensed. Evelyn's eyes widened with understanding of Sam's intent. "Don't you dare."

I drew a deep breath, held it for a count of five, then blew it out. This was not going to end well, but I saw no other way. I had to talk to Evelyn. I met Liz's gaze. "I need to have a private conversation with your guardian angel, but she won't leave your side."

"Damn you, Grim," Evelyn growled. Guardian angels were supposed to operate in the background—always vigilant, but never seen. I'd just blown her cover.

Liz slumped back in her chair. Her expression shifted from exasperation to disbelief. "My *what*?"

"Guardian angel. Her name is Evelyn, a former captain of the Heavenly Host."

Liz's eyes narrowed. "And how would you know *that*, Frank?"

Cora put a warning hand on Liz's forearm. Her other hand clutched Abigail's Celtic cross necklace in a white-knuckled grip. "He's not Frank. It's a long story, but you're talking to the Grim Reaper trapped in Frank's body. He still looks and sounds like Frank, my ears keep telling my heart that it's him, but Frank is gone. I don't know about any guardian angels, but Grim here is the real deal." Cora eyed Sam and Inez, who didn't look surprised at this revelation, and she nodded to herself as if confirming a suspicion.

I grimaced at Cora, but I couldn't exactly complain that she'd blown my cover when I just did the same to Evelyn. Liz caught my expression, and I folded my arms. "I told you, death is always on my mind. I *am* the Grim Reaper."

There was a moment of tense silence before Liz abruptly burst out laughing. It was a bright, delighted laugh that tipped the room's tension on its head. She wiped her eyes, tried to talk, looked at our serious expressions, then devolved into laughter again.

It was a while before Liz gasped between breaths, "Well done! You almost had me. I've heard of weird initiation pranks, but *man* you guys take the cake!" Girlish giggles escaped her, and she covered her mouth.

Anger radiated off Evelyn. I met her gaze over Liz's shoulder and said, "Please, Evelyn. I need your help. I wouldn't ask if it weren't a matter of grave importance. The Auditor's minions are stealing souls and bypassing Judgment."

Evelyn's shoulders tensed for a moment before they sagged, and she swore. It wasn't blasphemous, but I doubt Gabriel would have approved. Evelyn moved to the foot of the table like a stalking panther. If she'd had a tail, it would have been twitching furiously. She clutched the back of the empty chair, spread her ink-black wings, then turned corporeal and revealed herself.

Chapter 28

THE DEPTHS OF ABADDON

LIZ'S REACTION WAS PROFOUND. Her giggles cut off with a yelp when Evelyn revealed herself. She lurched aside, knocking over her chair. Cora, who looked only slightly less shocked, tried to catch her, but Liz dropped to the floor. She scurried up behind Cora's chair, dark curls falling in front of her face. She pointed a shaking finger at Evelyn.

"How ... you ... *holy shit*!" Liz's gaze flicked from side to side, taking in Evelyn's full wingspan.

Evelyn's glower at me softened into a smirk for Liz. "Nice to meet you too. I'm Evelyn, and I've been guarding you for twenty years." She folded her wings and extended a hand.

My eyebrows rose. Evelyn had been free of Abaddon for two decades?

Liz gulped, wiped her palms on her pants, then shook her guardian angel's hand. I glanced around the table. Cora looked shocked; her hand pressed to her chest. Inez leaned forward excitedly while Sam merely sat back with his arms crossed.

I cleared my throat. "Now that we have the pleasantries out of the way, allow me to explain."

Evelyn retrieved Liz's chair, gestured for her to sit, then took the empty chair at the foot of the table.

Once everyone was settled, I told Evelyn what had happened, leaving nothing out.

Well, almost nothing. I managed to talk around the bit about Abigail, Cora's daughter, being trapped in Torments. That isn't the kind of news a mother would take well. As much as Cora had been fingering that Celtic cross she'd gotten from Abigail, I knew that her daughter was on her mind. No need to add to her suffering.

When I finished, Evelyn sat back and shook her head.

"No. I'm not helping you kill the Auditor just to buy you time."

"But—"

"Yes, he's crossed the line by stealing souls, but that's for Heaven to solve, not you. You're just trying to win your feud."

"Damn it, Evelyn! This isn't about me! Humanity itself is at risk. Just like at Megiddo. But, unlike that fateful day, the solution here is simple. You are not bound by the Rules. You can kill the Auditor and save more souls from being dragged straight to Hell!"

Evelyn rocked forward, fire in her eyes. "But at what cost? You didn't pay the price at Megiddo. *I* did!" She slapped the table between us. "Five *thousand* years I rotted in Abaddon! Because of you."

"But you escaped..." Even as I said it, I knew it was the wrong thing.

"Oh, and that makes it better?"

"Evelyn, I'm sorry—"

"You don't know what it was like." Anguish twisted her face. "Abaddon is a pit of pure darkness. No light, nothing to even strike a spark. Yet it is more than a great pit. Endless caves and tunnels wind through the rock, shifting and changing so that the spirits damned to roam Abaddon's halls are forever lost in the depths of darkness."

Breaths caught around the table, but I didn't dare look away from Evelyn. Liz laid a hand on her wrist. Evelyn trembled at the touch before pulling away and folding her arms. Her wings curled protectively around her own shoulders, and her gaze focused on the table's center.

Cora pointed at me while giving Evelyn a concerned look. "He abandoned you to *literal* Hell? And I thought my ex was an ass!" She folded her arms in a mirror of Evelyn's posture and turned the full heat of her glare on me.

Evelyn just stared glassy eyed at the table. When she spoke, her rough voice was low.

"I evaded the Hell-spawn for a time, perhaps a century or two, before they caught me. I won't tell you what they did, but Nigel's reputation for cruelty was well-earned."

"Nigel?" Liz asked quietly.

"King of the Demigods. I don't know how long he tortured me. Centuries at least. Anger kept me sane. Anger at you"—she glanced at me—"at Gabriel, at the Almighty himself." She shuddered. "Well, perhaps not sane, but it provided an anchor when I lost myself. Then, one day, my salvation came from an unexpected quarter. One of Nigel's spawn freed me; a wretched Cambion who was more human than demon. I was surprised, but not about to refuse such a gift."

My brows furrowed. "Why did he save you?"

"He begged for mercy. For *Mercy*." She touched the sword's hilt, which was just visible above the table's edge. "Nigel had taken the blade when I was captured, and together we stole it back. For the Cambion's help, I granted his wish." She'd unmade him. Evelyn drew a ragged breath. "After that, I became the hunter, determined to rid Abaddon's cursed halls of Hell's darkest creations."

"And did you?" I asked.

"Almost. After five millennia, Nigel alone eluded me."

Silence fell, and I drummed my fingers on the table. Diana chose that moment to jump into my lap with an insistent purr. She pressed herself under my hands, and I scratched behind her ears. Evelyn's tormented expression softened when she saw the cat. Despite her protests to the contrary, she'd always loved cats. She reached out and let Diana sniff her fingers before scratching the cat under her jaw.

"And now the King of the Demigods is free from Abaddon," I said. "I saw him yesterday pretending to be a human politician named Damien Nigel."

Cora cursed under her breath and shook her head. "I can't believe I voted for him."

"How is it that you are both free?" I asked Evelyn.

She drew a ragged breath and met my gaze. Pain filled her dark eyes. "I wanted to kill Nigel, but he'd found the way to freedom. He dug himself out of Abaddon, patiently picking at a weak spot he'd found in the rift that *you* opened."

My eyes narrowed. "You made a deal with a Demigod and judge *me* for keeping company with demons? Alvin went into a tailspin after you attacked him!"

Evelyn's jaw clenched. "There is good, and there is evil. Demons are evil. Shades of gray are merely light tainted with darkness."

"You make my point."

"I know! It was wrong, but I was weak. I ... I couldn't find another way. After all that time in darkness..." She shuddered. "Yet, somehow, after my escape, the Almighty saw fit to forgive me. He even gave me a new mission, despite my failure. To become a guardian."

She glanced at Liz. The girl's eyes brimmed with tears, and she turned her outstretched hand palm up, offering comfort. Evelyn took the hand and squeezed it. Liz's throat worked as though she wanted to speak. No words came.

I ran my fingers down Diana's sides and considered Evelyn's story. Little tufts of white fur floated up, drifting to join the demon-lettuce on my plate. The cat's rumbling purr sounded loud in the silent dining room. I looked at Cora, Sam, and Inez, but they only exchanged glances.

This was *my* moment with Evelyn, my opportunity to make amends for her millennia of suffering.

I cleared my throat. "I'm sorry for the pain I caused you. You're right. I cannot imagine what it was like, and I won't beg for forgiveness that you can't give. Just know that if I can ever make amends, I will. Whatever you ask."

Evelyn's eyes tightened. "If you want to make amends, stop Nigel. Send him back to Abaddon and throw away the key. I don't know what scheme he's hatching by playing a human politician, but it can't be good. If you can do that, we'll talk about forgiveness."

My fingers paused on Diana's spine. "And in exchange, you'll kill the Auditor?"

She shook her head. "No. I'm a guardian now. I can't leave Liz."

Damn.

"Why?" I asked. "No offense to Liz, but what makes her so important to the Almighty?"

Evelyn grimaced. "You know that's not how He works. He deals in riddles and prophesies, not straight answers—"

Cora snorted. "Preach it, sister!"

"—so all I got was a vague impression that Liz was important to some future event."

Liz rolled her eyes. "Like I'm some chosen one? No, thank you! I've seen how those movies end."

Evelyn shook her head. "I only know that you will play an important role. You could be destined for greatness, or you could provide something that catapults someone else to great deeds. Small actions often have big effects that you never see."

"Oh, how profound!" a voice said from the kitchen. A voice as dry as crumpled ash that dripped with cultured menace. Sam and I spun toward the kitchen while Evelyn leapt up and drew *Mercy.*

The others froze, uncertainty on their faces. Only we three could see the demon who rose through the white-tiled floor as if riding an elevator. He was tall and impossibly gaunt, like stretched dough, and wore the archetypical demon's rumpled suit. Gold-rimmed spectacles covered blood-red eyes which narrowed at Evelyn and *Mercy* before scanning the faces in the room. Claws drummed on the back of an oversized clipboard. My blood ran cold.

The Auditor had found me.

THE AUDITOR

How? How had the Auditor found me?

That question was answered when Xandu rose through the tile beside the Auditor, broad and powerful and still missing his left forearm.

Of course. I was such a fool. Xandu must have identified Inez at the Grand Estates and traced her to her home through their records. He drew his remaining scimitar and pointed it at me. Murder glinted in the brute's blood-red eyes, and his voice rumbled like thunder.

"There he is. Frank Totmann, the one who thought he could get away."

The Auditor nodded. "So I see. And look what other treasure we've found. *Mercy* and the elusive Evelyn. Nigel will be pleased." He withdrew a cheap ballpoint from his suit and made two tick marks on his oversized clipboard. "Take *Mercy* and deliver it to Nigel. The lost soul is mine." He pointed the ballpoint pen my way, "Frank Totmann, your time is come."

Pandemonium erupted. It was a mix of confusion and fear as only half of us could see and hear the demons. They hadn't revealed themselves to the mortal realm. Everyone jumped up and several things happened simultaneously.

Diana hissed and scrambled off my lap, claws gouging into my legs.

Sam grabbed Inez's hand and pulled her aside, leaving only an empty chair between the Auditor and me.

Cora yanked her iron Celtic cross from around her neck and thrust it toward the kitchen like one of the saints brandishing a holy relic. "Get back, demon!" Clearly, she'd figured out some of what was going on.

The Auditor ignored her. Xandu scrunched his nose at the talisman.

Evelyn, still corporeal, pushed Liz toward the front door with one hand and placed herself and *Mercy* between the demons and her charge.

"What's going on?" Liz asked, eyes darting about wildly.

I found myself on my feet and answered around the lump in my throat. "The Auditor has come for my soul."

The Auditor's eyes narrowed when I named him.

Inez swore and let Sam push her toward the front door. I could tell that she wanted to fight, to defend her home, but she wasn't equipped for this battle. She couldn't see the enemy. Sam drew his blessed letter opener and stood shoulder-to-shoulder between Evelyn and Cora. *Faith, Mercy,* and an unknown Celtic bauble formed a defensive line.

I was on the wrong side of that line and on the wrong side of the table.

The Auditor lumbered forward and ducked into the dining room, his curled horns passing just under the arched doorway. He stepped through Sam's chair and the edge of the table, a spirit not bothered by inconvenient laws of physics.

I had no such freedom. I scrambled around the table toward the defenders and slipped behind them.

Evelyn lunged toward the Auditor, *Mercy* stabbing forward. The Auditor's oversized clipboard swung down like a shield, and *Mercy*'s tip slid off its back with a scrape of sparks. Evelyn twisted the blade, shifted her stance, and sliced downward. This time the clipboard caught Evelyn's blade solidly and a hollow *boom* of impact shook the room.

Evelyn stepped back, eyes wide. I too was surprised. I'd never considered the Auditor's clipboard as anything more than a home for his checklists and papers.

It was more. So much more. An infernal shield forged in the Lake of Fire. I should have known.

Cora twisted wildly from side to side, holding her cross out like a shield of her own. "I can't see them! Where are they?"

Evelyn kept her gaze fixed on the Auditor but reached over and placed a hand over Cora's eyes. When she removed her hand, Cora flinched back. Evelyn had opened Cora's third eye. Already-wide eyes bulged, but she swung the cross toward the Auditor and Xandu.

Xandu roared and charged, scimitar drawn. Evelyn slipped ahead of Cora, and *Mercy* blocked his blade with an electric crackle. Once. Twice. Three times they clashed in under a second. Lightning flashed with each strike, raising the hair on my neck. The Auditor stepped into the corner where I'd been sitting to avoid the flashing blades as the two fought. I remained behind the shield wall of my companions, weaponless and helpless to assist.

Cora snarled at Xandu when he stepped close to her. "I said get back, demon!" The iron cross slipped from her grasp and dropped the length of its chain which was hooked on Cora's middle finger. She spun the relic like a sling and whipped it at Xandu's face.

To my shock—and his—the cross struck Xandu's cheek as if he were a physical being and stuck. Black smoke sizzled around the cross.

That bauble actually *was* a holy relic.

Xandu screamed.

He lurched back and the cross popped off his face, dropping with a jangle of chain to Cora's side. Righteous fury glowed in her eyes, and she spun the cross again. Evelyn lunged forward and together they pushed Xandu back into the kitchen.

The Auditor, who'd stood in the corner like the world's most terrifying statue, stepped forward. "Enough games, Frank Totmann. Your time is come!"

Sam stepped between us, brandishing *Faith*. The Auditor paused again, lips pursed.

Liz and Inez, who could only see half of the raging

battle, huddled beside me. I pointed Inez toward the door. "This is not your fight. Take Liz and run!" I hissed.

Inez bit her lip but nodded. She pulled Liz back and within a second they were out the door.

The Auditor loomed over Sam, brows furrowed. "I remember you, Samuel Davidson."

"Yeah, I'm pretty hard to forget." Sam's voice was crisp and full of bravado.

The Auditor's thin face pulsed as his jaw clenched. "You are not today's problem ... but know this. I *will* address your betrayal. Personally."

That wasn't good. I still didn't know what the hell had happened between Sam and Alvin, but the Auditor wasn't as clueless as Sam had thought.

The Auditor pocketed his pen and pointed a clawed finger at me. "But first I must reap this man's soul."

Sam's crouch tightened. I backed into the entry hall, ready to run through the door Inez had left open. I had no weapons, no defense beyond Sam. The Auditor tried stepping around Sam, but my protector lunged forward with a yell. *Faith* slashed toward the demon's heart.

As if the Auditor *had* a heart.

The lanky demon leaned aside and whipped his clipboard around. The flat of it struck both the letter opener and Sam's wrist, ringing like an iron shield. Sam stumbled, his momentum carrying him forward, and the Auditor slammed the clipboard into Sam's wrist again—with the edge this time. I heard the crack of bone.

Sam screamed. *Faith* clattered to the floor and slid toward me. I scooped it up. Sam stumbled back, clutching a broken wrist. The Auditor grinned, revealing sharp teeth.

"Consider that a taste of things to come, Samuel Davidson. We'll talk soon." The clipboard whipped out in a backhand strike that smashed into Sam's temple. He flew into the table, scattering dishes and kale with a clatter before he collapsed limply to the floor.

The Auditor's blood-red eyes turned toward me. He adjusted his gold-wire glasses. "Now it's your turn, Frank Totmann."

I spun toward the front door, but the Auditor beat me to it. He kicked the door shut with a boom that made the house shudder. My jaw clenched. What I wouldn't give to have such freedom to pick and choose when to let the laws of physics affected me. But all I could do was clutch *Faith* and back into the living room.

Evelyn and Cora still fought Xandu in the attached

kitchen. The spirits slid through and around cabinets and the kitchen island, blades flashing with lightning while Cora struck from the sidelines any time Xandu came close. Red cross-shaped welts decorated the demon's face and skin-tight suit.

The Auditor stalked after me. Could I keep him distracted long enough for Evelyn to slay both Xandu and him?

No. Despite only having one arm, Xandu was holding his own against both Evelyn and Cora. I had to deal with the Auditor myself.

At least now I had *Faith*, a blessed blade that only required the smallest cut to banish a demon back to Hell.

I stabbed as a feint. The Auditor swung his clipboard to block, and I shortened my attack. The clipboard whipped past, and I sliced at his arm.

I missed.

The Auditor backhanded me with the clipboard so hard that my feet left the ground. I spun through the air and flew over the couch to crash facedown into the shag carpet on its far side. *Faith* flew from my fingers.

I gasped, drawing ragged breaths. Under the couch, Diana's green eyes shone at me. She hissed.

A clawed hand gripped my shoulder. The Auditor rolled me onto my back, and he grinned. "Frank Totmann, you were supposed to die four days ago. Your continued existence is an anomaly that must be corrected."

Evelyn's scream whipped both our gazes toward the kitchen. We looked past the side of the couch. White gaseous essence of angel wafted from a long cut across Evelyn's chest, stark white against her black leather vest. Xandu stood in a samurai's pose, blade high after delivering the killing blow.

"No!" I yelled.

Evelyn dropped to her knees. Cora stood frozen in shock before she dropped her cross and rushed to Evelyn's side. She tried to staunch the wound, but her fingers passed through the angel's chest. Evelyn began to fade, banished to Heaven in accordance with the Rules.

I'd been wrong. Evelyn *was* bound by the Rules.

Xandu dropped his scimitar and reached past the kneeling Cora to snatch *Mercy*. Evelyn caught my gaze, and her lips formed Elizabeth's name as she disappeared, though no words came out. Her charge was now unguarded. If Hell discovered Liz's importance to Heaven, they'd be after her next.

Xandu met the Auditor's gaze and raised his prize with a roar of victory.

Cora screamed in fury and threw herself at the demon. She passed straight through him and crashed into the counter. Desperately, she cast about for her cross.

"Go," the Auditor said to Xandu, his ash-dry voice purring with pleasure. "Deliver *Mercy* to Nigel with my compliments." Xandu nodded and sank into the floor.

Cora found her cross and threw it with a yell. Xandu ducked aside, and the cross clattered harmlessly against the oven door before he disappeared.

An evil chuckle rumbled from the Auditor's chest. "That little gift just secured my position in Hell's new order."

New order? What new order?

The Auditor continued as if he'd heard me. "A new order where *I* am Death, Judge, and Executioner!" He thrust a clawed hand into my chest.

Searing cold washed through me. I'm not a praying man. A praying spirit? Being? Whatever! The point is, I've never had a great relationship with the Almighty, but death makes believers of all men, as the saying goes.

"God, help me!" I screamed.

God did not answer.

Diana did.

The cat flew out from under the couch in a ball of white-furred savagery. Her war cry warbled like a lion's. Diana slammed into the Auditor, knocking him off me. She shouldn't have been able to touch him, not if he didn't want her to, but that didn't seem to matter.

Apparently, cats can defy the laws of physics as easily as demons.

The Auditor fell onto his back, and I gasped as his claws released my chest. He smacked at Diana with his clipboard, but he may as well have hit her with feathers for all that she noticed. Diana swarmed up the Auditor's chest and bit the side of his neck.

He cursed, that bone-dry voice sounding surprised and slightly panicked.

I scrabbled out of the way, stopping only when my back hit the television stand. The Auditor rolled, trying to dislodge the cat, but Diana just landed on the carpet and dug in, her teeth still firmly attached to the side of his neck.

Then, to my amazement, Diana started to pull the Auditor back toward the couch. He struggled, fought against her, but the physical cat was more powerful than a spiritual demon.

Who knew?

Diana backed herself under the couch, yanking and pulling the Auditor with her with chest deep growls. From my angle, I could see under the couch, and I watched as she slunk backward toward its corner. Then Diana did something I'd never witnessed.

She crossed over to Hell and dragged the Auditor with her.

Diana's transition to the infernal realm looked like a whirlpool spiraling into an unstopped drain. It was a silent whirlpool, for cats wouldn't have it any other way. Her tail went first, followed by hips, shoulders, and head, all spiraling down into whatever gateway existed for cats in the hidden places that they love. The Auditor spun into the vortex in a flopping flail of limbs and clipboard which squeezed impossibly narrow as he was pulled into a singular point of nothingness. The Auditor's screech of indignant anger cut off abruptly when his last clawed toe disappeared.

Silence filled the house.

Chapter 30

DEATH

I STARED AT THE empty space under the couch and sucked relieved breaths.

"Grim?" Cora said from the kitchen. "Are you okay?"

A half-smile stole over my face as I clambered to my feet. "I thought you didn't care."

"That was before I saw…" She waved, the gesture somehow encompassing the entire battle we'd just fought. "I'm still pissed at you for taking my Abigail, but if Hell really is your enemy, then I'm your ally." Her eyes lingered on the spot where Evelyn had disappeared. She shuddered and retrieved her cross, wrapping it so that the iron lay over her knuckles.

Cora crossed to the living room, that same look of gentle compassion on her face that she'd had when I first met her. Back when she'd thought I was Frank. She touched my face where the Auditor's clipboard had hit me. I flinched, and she asked, "Is it over?"

I shook my head. "No. The Auditor will return the second he escapes Diana's claws." And he wouldn't stop until he had my soul. He didn't know my true identity, but I'd pissed him off. This was personal now.

As if on cue, the Auditor rose again through the kitchen floor in a firestorm of red lightning that would have made Alvin proud. Electricity arced from floor to ceiling, bouncing and rebounding off cabinets and appliances until the hair on my arms stood on end. "Frank Totmann!" the Auditor yelled, straining his normal ash-dry wheeze. "Your soul is mine!"

I cast about but couldn't see where *Faith* had fallen. Cora pulled her fist back, ready to strike with cold iron.

I placed a hand on her shoulder. The Auditor had bested Sam without breaking a sweat. He would destroy her. "Thank you," I said to Cora, "but this is not your fight. He cannot hurt you if I am gone."

I squeezed Cora's shoulder and took the only option remaining to me.

I ran.

***

Evading the Auditor was simple, yet terribly difficult. I had to abandon every resource I had. The lumbering demon gave chase, but his skills lay in tracking through files and records, not in active pursuit. I lost him after several heart-wrenching hours by squeezing behind a strip mall dumpster.

I had nowhere to go. I had to avoid Frank's house. Cora. The Land of Evil Auditors. Anywhere that might connect me to Frank's life or the people in it. The Auditor had proven that he could track me through even distant associates. I'd brought Hell to the Davidson household. They were lovely people who didn't deserve the pain and terror I'd caused them.

I woke with a start the following morning. I'd been having a nightmare of fleeing the Auditor through a maze of doors, each with its own bloody different handle. I blinked sleep-laden eyes. Realization dawned slowly that I was not actually trapped in that dream-maze. I lay on cold cement, pressed between a dumpster that smelled like something had died in it and a brick wall blackened with grime. Orange-dappled clouds drifted overhead, visible through the gap between dumpster and building. I hadn't felt sleep sneak up as the temperature dropped.

Friday. The end of the work week. Would I make it to Saturday?

I squeezed out of my hiding place and into a parking lot, stamping warmth into my tingling toes. My joints protested; cold muscles so tight that I could barely walk. Frank's black pinstripe suit was tattered and stained. I shielded my eyes against the low sun. I didn't know where I was.

An unfortunately familiar pressure made me grimace. Alvin's fourth incessant need had found me yet again. I trudged across the parking lot toward a gas station. A bell tinkled as I entered and warm air washed over me, inducing a wave of relaxation.

Heavens, that felt good.

The pressure on my bowels intensified.

"Toilet?" I asked the lanky teen behind the counter. He pointed to the back without looking up from his phone. I followed his vague directions, found the toilet, and once again succumbed to mortality's dark side. The little re-stroom lacked soap, but I scrubbed my hands until the skin was raw, then fled.

The bell chimed again as I left. The wind struck me as I stepped outside and I stopped, huddled in on myself, not sure where to go next.

"Grim?"

I jumped and turned toward the voice, ready to run. Louis the cabbie waved from behind a car he was fueling. Not his cab, but a beat-up green sedan.

"Brother, you look awful," he said. "What happened?"

I snorted. "How much time do you have?"

Louis's eyebrows rose. "That bad, huh?"

I shrugged. "My past ... caught up with me."

"Who? The guy who stole from you on Monday?"

It took me a moment to realize that he was referring to Frank. I shook my head. "No. A Hell-spawned demon called the Auditor. He ... you wouldn't understand."

Louis stepped around his car, concern in his gray eyes. "I understand the look of a man running from his mistakes. Everything looks bad when you're in the middle of it. I couldn't see a way out of my problems with Nicole until I talked to you. You were right, time was what Nicole needed. My time. We're going on an actual date tonight. To Edelweiss, if you'd believe it!"

I grunted. "Have the Apfelstrudel. It's to die for."

Louis chuckled and held out a hand. "Come on, let me take you to breakfast. You'll see things clearer with a full stomach and some caffeine."

My stomach rumbled. "Thank you. Your generosity is—"

An iron vise seized my chest and my breath wheezed out. I dropped to the pavement, struggling for air, muscles turning watery. Frank's traitorous heart seized again, sending a spike through the vise.

"Grim!" Louis knelt beside me, a hand on my back. "What's wrong?"

"Heart ... attack. Third in ... five days."

"Hey!" he yelled at the kid inside. "Give me a hand!"

I grabbed his arm. "Please ... don't let me die." My heart beat rapidly as if to make up for lost time, taunting me with hope.

"Hold on, Grim. You're not dying today."

I collapsed. Rough pavement scratched my face, and my brain turned fuzzy. Strong arms lifted me to lay across Louis's back seat. The door slammed, the engine started, and we tore out of the lot.

The world became snapshots of consciousness as Louis wove through traffic, blaring his horn. Anxious assurances washed over me while I struggled to survive. To live. Reversing Frank's Sumerian soul-swapping spell was a distant desire. Avoiding the Auditor was more immediate.

Would he recognize my soul this time as he ripped it out? Would it make a difference to my fate?

"No hospital," I wheezed, but Louis didn't hear me. A hospital would put Frank's name on record. The Auditor would see it.

We screeched to a stop, Louis yelled for help, and more hands pulled me from the car.

"What happened?" a woman asked in a no-nonsense tone as they laid me on a gurney. I struggled to recognize her voice. Lisle. Nurse Candice Lisle.

"Heart attack," Louis said, "Third in five days."

"And he's still breathing? Death's not ready for this guy. What's his name?"

"Grim Reaper."

"*Not* the time for jokes." Nurse Lisle's voice turned severe. Hands dug through my pockets. Lint and Beatrix's tombstone-shaped masterpiece went flying. My heart lurched. I tried to grab the little scrap, to save the only gift I'd ever received, but my hand flopped uselessly. Nurse Lisle found Frank's wallet. "Says Frank Totmann on his license."

No. Please. I reached for the wallet, but someone grabbed my arm and placed it back on the gurney.

Nurse Lisle's eyes widened and flicked to my face. "Sweet Mother Mary," she whispered. "You're overseeing my tax audit." I tried to speak, to apologize, to beg, to say something that my muddled brain couldn't articulate, but she just shook her head and leaned close. "Don't worry. You're in good hands."

They wheeled me inside. Lights flashed past overhead as nurses rushed me ... somewhere. We pushed into a brightly lit room that smelled of antiseptic and was filled with stainless steel counters and medical devices on little carts. Louis's anxious face peered through the windowed door, his lips moving with silent prayer.

Pain exploded in my chest, and I screamed. My eyes bulged and I squeezed a hand I found in mine.

"Crash cart, now!" someone yelled—

Time stopped so abruptly that I felt jolted out of reality.

The pain ... paused. The room's flurry of activity froze

midmotion. I sagged, drawing ragged breaths.

Frank glided through the wall, smirking from the depths of my cowl, my scythe in hand. "Dying sucks, huh?" he said.

Cheeky, insufferable, little son of a...

I sat up and gauged the distance between us. "You toy with powers you don't understand, Frank Totmann."

"I'm figuring it out. The stopping time thing is pretty cool. Last night I played a round of golf with a dying CEO before sending him on his way." He twirled my scythe then pretended to putt.

"You are supposed to grant an opportunity for confession. Not ... play golf." I shook my head, appalled, and swiveled my legs off the table.

Frank swung the scythe back into a two-handed grip and ducked behind a nurse frozen in frantic motion. He narrowed his eyes at me. "It's been a bit longer for me, what with stopping time, but I figured you'd have more than five days. How'd you like being human?"

"It was terrifying, confusing, and ... enjoyable. I found your fellow humans thoughtful and kind. I had a date with Cora."

Frank's eyes went wide. "Ah, crap. I forgot about that. I

meant to cancel."

"She helped you prepare. You didn't tell her your plan?"

He bit one lip and said, "I couldn't. Didn't want to see her cry. She's gonna be heartbroken when I die. Well, when you die."

"Everybody leaves loved ones behind. We all have unfinished business."

His grip tightened on *Grace*, and he nodded, stepping back around the nurse. "Well, I guess it's time. Best of luck in the afterlife!" He pulled the scythe back, readying the Reaper's power over the soul.

Realization hit me so hard that I almost fell off the gurney. My breath caught. I didn't need to reverse Frank's Sumerian spell. I needed my scythe. *Grace* didn't just sever souls from their mortal coil. It created balance, moving souls to where they were supposed to be.

I was supposed to be in that cowl and Frank in this body.

I held up a hand. "Wait! You can't reap me."

Frank's eyes narrowed, my death over his shoulder, my salvation in his hands. "Why not?"

"The Auditor is coming for you."

Fear crept into Frank's voice. "The who?"

"The Auditor. Hell's final arbiter of the Rules. Hell

noticed discrepancies after you took my place. The Auditor hates discrepancies and metes out punishment with ... finality." Frank lowered the scythe and glanced around furtively.

"I'm not taking my body back. I already cheated death."

Yes, you were the first. I will be the second.

I leaned forward conspiratorially. "Here's what we'll—"

The words froze in my throat as the Auditor lurched through the door. Claws scratched angry gouges on the back of his clipboard as he pointed it at me. "Frank Totmann, your—"

He noticed the real Frank Totmann, and his brows bunched together behind gold-wire frames. "Two Frank Totmanns?" He consulted his clipboard and growled, "This is highly irregular." He considered me and then Frank, who made the mistake of meeting his gaze.

Tension drained from the Auditor's shoulders. He stood up straight and adjusted his glasses. "There you are. Your Judgment is at hand." He eyed the scythe, then me. I saw connections click in his evil mind. A dark smile stole over the Auditor's gaunt face. "Ah, it all makes sense now. You have failed, Grim. It's time to face your Judgment, too. It's time for a new Reaper." He turned to Frank. "I'll start with this impostor's soul."

Frank stumbled backward, lip quivering. "No!"

I jumped off the gurney. "Give me the scythe!"

"No!" Panic tainted Frank's words, and the Auditor lunged at him. Frank leapt between two nurses and the Auditor followed, implacable. They danced around my gurney, just out of reach. I had to do something. Anything to keep the Auditor from *Grace*.

"Wait!" I yelled and leapt between them, throwing my hands out like a referee separating boxers. Frank scrambled back, but the Auditor thrust a long-fingered hand into my chest. He gripped my soul.

Cold washed through me, and I felt myself dying all over again. My breath wheezed. Frank's wide eyes met mine, and I turned my palm up, beseeching.

"Please, before he drags us both into Hell with him."

Frank's gaze whipped to the Auditor who yanked at my soul, half tearing it from my body. I screamed and collapsed to my knees.

Frank shook his head.

In that moment, as every nerve ending in my body screamed in agony, I realized that I'd misjudged Frank Totmann. He wasn't an evil mastermind. He was just a man.

Scared of death, yet infinitely resourceful.

But could I trust him? Could he trust *me*?

Time to find out.

"I'll ... make you an apprentice!"

"But..."

"Or you die!"

Frank quivered, then nodded and thrust *Grace* into my hands.

Power flowed into me. Power to stop time and parse souls. Power over life itself. I smelled the cherry blossoms of Heaven and the burning sulfur of Hell, an intoxicating brew that overwhelmed my pain.

I spun on my knees to slam the scythe into the Auditor's chest, but he caught the handle with a crack. Lightning surged around his grip, and he tried to yank *Grace* away.

He failed.

"You are not Death," I intoned. "You never will be."

I rose, scythe between us, and shed Frank Totmann's skin and tattered suit. They drifted away like flaming embers that pushed onto Frank's terrified soul, leaving me a proud, naked skeleton. The embers solidified and Frank became flesh once more. I shrouded my skeletal form in a cowled cloak of darkness drawn from Hell itself.

I was Death.

I kicked the Auditor in the chest and wrenched my scythe away. He flew through a frozen nurse and the wall with a furious roar. He'd be back.

I spun and pointed an accusing finger. "Frank Totmann, you cannot run from Death."

"Wait, what? No! You said …" He fell back and bumped into the crash cart, making the wheels squeak. I placed my blade to his throat, and a sob escaped him. "Please, I don't want to die."

"I understand," I whispered, and I did. I really did. He squeezed his eyes shut and pressed back. I swung my scythe and reaped Frank's soul. His body collapsed, and his spirit bobbed into the ether beside me. I gripped his shoulder to keep him in place and turned as the Auditor stormed in.

"Frank Totmann is dead," I said. "The scales are balanced; the Rules are satisfied. You have nothing further to audit here."

The Auditor glanced at Frank's soul, then at *Grace* clutched firmly in my bony grip. Raw desire and bitter realization burned in his red eyes. The Rules forbade interfering with Death's duties, and the Auditor was more bound to the Rules than I. The loophole created by

Frank's spell had just closed.

"Damn you." His fists clenched. "Where will you send him?"

"Not your concern. And neither are the other souls awaiting my attention. The Office of Micromanagement's brief jurisdiction over the souls of the living is over." I'd need to do something about the souls he'd already stolen, but that problem would have to wait.

The Auditor cursed and retrieved his clipboard. He made a definitive checkmark, which sounded like it tore through parchment. "I'm watching you, Grim," he said.

"And I you." My eye sockets flared bright with flame. "Death, Judge, *and* Executioner? You always did over-reach."

"Change is coming," the Auditor growled. "Hell's Bureaucracy will burn, and Nigel's New Order will rise." He leaned forward, ash-dry voice fervent. "And there's nothing you can do to stop it!" He sneered and then spun on his heel to stomp away through the wall.

Nigel's New Order? Something told me that was going to be a problem. A big one. But it wasn't today's problem. I had more pressing matters.

I counted to twenty to ensure that the Auditor was

gone before starting time again. A cacophony of noise and action burst into the room.

The nurses scrambled, confused to find Frank's body beside the crash cart. Nurse Lisle checked his vitals, sagged, then declared him dead.

Frank looked up as they carted his body away. "You killed me."

"No, your body died. I retrieved your soul. A minor, but important distinction."

"Now what? Were you serious about making me an apprentice?"

I rubbed my chin and reveled in its bony lack of beard. "I could use the company. And you've proven quite re-sourceful. For a human."

He sighed, relief twitching the corners of his lips. "All right, Boss, what first? Do I get my own scythe?"

I gave him a flaming stare. "First, we correct your errors from the past week. There are souls who need to pass on. For failing at your assumed duties, you must take their confessions."

"But I didn't know what I was doing!"

"That's no excuse. Every soul deserves your utmost care. Come, I will show you." I paused and glanced at his tattered pinstriped suit. "But you can't go reaping souls look-ing like *that*. We have a certain image to uphold." I held firmly onto Frank's shoulder and concentrated on *Grace*. On drawing things to where they needed to be.

A cloaked cowl from the depths of Hell materialized around Frank's shoulders. It was a perfect mirror of mine but sized to fit Frank's more robust frame.

Much better. With nothing else to hold us here, Frank and I followed the incessant pull of a soul in need of tran-sition.

Chapter 31

LUCY'S LAST DAY

I WAS NOT SURPRISED to discover that Lucy Pembrook was the next soul in need of transition.

Frank and I found Lucy at her desk in the Land of Evil Auditors, talking on her phone. Her cubicle was neat and orderly—I'd expected nothing less—with only a single manila folder open upon the desk. The cubicle farm was empty, it was early yet, but Lucy's cheerful voice filled the large room.

"Yes, Mr. Lisle," she said into the phone. "Your wife sent all the documents, and your audit is now complete." There was a pause. "Actually, the IRS owes you. $2,182 to be exact." Pause. "It was my pleasure, no trouble at all. I'll send it over as soon as it's signed." There was another pause, and Lucy smiled warmly at whatever Mr. Lisle had said. She chuckled and said, "You too. Take care," and hung up.

I stopped time just before Lucy's fatal stroke. Her hand was still poised over the phone. Her gaze flicked over her shoulder at me as I appeared. I pointed a bony finger, prepared to intone, then paused.

Old habits die hard. This was Frank's reaping, not mine. I nudged him with an elbow.

Lucy spun in her chair and eyed Frank in his reaper's cowl. She glanced at me with a flash of confusion but focused on Frank. "It's a bit early for Halloween, Frank, but I'm glad you're here. I just finished the Lisle audit, and it needs your final review before I sign."

Frank glanced at me, and I let my eye sockets flame a bit for effect. "Go on," I intoned. "You know what to do."

Frank nodded, cleared his throat, and extended a pudgy finger. "Lucy Pembrook, your time is come." He still sounded like a squeaky bureaucrat, but we could work on that. Lucy glanced back at me and met my fiery gaze.

Her expression shifted from annoyed to surprised, to

angry.

Ah, there it was. That moment when the soul realized what was actually happening. That Death had come to call.

"Shit," she said. Her gaze flicked between us, and finally settled on my scythe. I twitched *Grace* slightly, so the blade reflected the harsh fluorescent lights. Lucy glared at Frank. "If I'm dead, what are *you* doing here?"

Frank looked less confident than I'd expected, but he squared his shoulders. "I, uh, died too. But I'm an apprentice Reaper now. I'm here to take your confession and then send you to the afterlife."

Not bad. He needed more dramatic flair, but again, that was something we could work on. I nodded solemnly when Lucy glanced at me for confirmation. Her lips pursed, and she retrieved a pen. "First, you need to review the Lisle audit so I can sign it. Otherwise, it'll get lost for months before someone is reassigned to it."

Normally, I would have forbidden any after-death interference with the mortal world. Death is final and everyone has tasks left undone. But I felt I owed something to Nurse Lisle. She hadn't saved me, but she'd damned well tried. Closing this painful chapter in her life was a little something I could give back. I nodded to Frank, and he grabbed the folder.

After a brief but intense scan of the Lisle audit, Frank nodded, and Lucy signed. When she finished, he fumbled through asking if Lucy had a final confession. She didn't, but seemed to want to reminisce. I stepped away to let them talk. As I waited, I considered the work week I'd just survived.

I shall forevermore hold a grudge against Mondays, for that was the traumatic day I became human. I am not cut out for mortality. It's dreadfully complicated and confusing. Yet, at the same time, I found my brief life surprisingly enjoyable.

Except for the dying.

And the defecation.

I experienced love, sorrow, joy, and pain. I found Evelyn, ever so briefly, but then lost her again. Despite all that she'd endured, Evelyn's banishment to Heaven was not a blessing. Heaven isn't as forgiving of angelic failures as one might expect. Look at what happened to me.

My bony brows knit together as I remembered Abigail's plight. Cora's daughter had been condemned to Torments without undergoing Judgment. Judgments were not my department, but I'd agreed to investigate her case. I'd given my word, and there's nothing more binding than the promise of Death. Nigel's New Order and the Auditor's Office of Micromanagement were behind this, I knew it. Proving it, however, was another matter.

But there was too much clean up to do first, too many souls awaiting Death's touch, to take the time Abigail's case needed. Besides, one did not just kick in Hell's front door and accuse upper management of violating the Rules. I would need to prepare. But once I did…

Death would come to Hell.

I eyed Frank as he chatted with Lucy on this, the last day of her life, and the first day of both their afterlives. If I was holding a grudge against Monday, then Friday would always hold a special place in my heart. Friday brought me an apprentice, whom I hope will eventually become a friend. It will be nice to have someone to share this lonely half-life with.

He would need a new name, though. "Death and Frank" lacked the proper authoritative ring.

I snapped my bony fingers, remembering. Frank already had a title. One that sparked fear and caution among the living. Together we would shepherd souls to their final rest as the two greatest certainties in life.

Death and the Taxman.

The adventure continues in *Death and the Dragon,* the wild ride through Hell that Dante wished he'd had.

Death and the Dragon

https://books2read.com/deathandthedragon

So, how did Sam get a blessed letter opener? What led
Cora to the dark arts? Did Evelyn really help Nigel escape
Abaddon? Read these stories and more in:

Grimsworld Tales

https://books2read.com/grimsworldtales

Thank you for reading *Death and the Taxman*!

Did you know that book reviews make authors go all soft and gooey inside?

It's true. We love hearing back from readers! Long or short doesn't matter, just share your thoughts.

If you would kindly leave a review on Amazon, Goodreads, or wherever you shop for books, you will have my eternal thanks.

Join the Lost Bard's Letter at https://davidhankins.com for more (free) lighthearted stories.

ACKNOWLEDGEMENTS

Death and the Taxman began as a short story, born as the writing community mourned the passing of Writers of the Future Coordinating Judge David Farland. It was my attempt to bring laughter in a time of grief. I was, of course, overjoyed when my silly story about Death won the biggest speculative fiction talent contest in the world, and I immediately dove head first into expanding that short story into a full-length novel. The novel you just finished reading. From *Death and the Taxman*'s inception to publication, I truly cannot count the people who helped in ways small and large.

First and foremost, I want to thank my wife Michelle and my daughter Beatrix for the years of unconditional support, both for my writing and for dealing with, well, me. Thank you for reading and listening to so many absolutely horrible first, second, and tenth drafts as I learned the art and craft of writing. *Death and the Taxman* would not have been possible without you.

My writing journey began long before I actually started *writing*. Mom, thank you for instilling in me a ravenous hunger for books, and for introducing me to the most magical world of all: the library.

To my writing mentor, Wulf Moon: thank you for paying it forward and selflessly giving of your time and knowledge to help so many writers achieve so much, so quickly. Without your Super Secrets of Writing, I would still be an enthusiastic amateur who drives to the story with choppy dialogue without setting my stage. And I wouldn't have a clue what to do with a magic sword.

A huge howling to the Wulf Pack Writers, the most amazing group of rogues and writers I've ever known. Thank you for all the critiques, support, and enthusiasm. I'm proud to run with the Pack!

To Scot and Jane Noel, editors of *DreamForge Magazine,* thank you for taking a chance on me and publishing my first short story, "A Properly Spiced Gingerbread." That first sale gave me the confidence to keep writing, to keep submitting, and to never quit.

So many thanks to Writers of the Future coordinating

judge Jody Lynn Nye and the other judges for selecting the original short story "Death and the Taxman" to win such a prestigious award and for publishing it in *Writers of the Future Volume 39* (May 2023). And thank you, Jody, for your kind words for my cover blurb. To John Goodwin and the amazing folks at Galaxy Press (who publish Writers of the Future), I am humbled and honored by your pay-it-forward attitude. Thank you for the ceaseless support.

Sarah Morrison, my illustrator ... words cannot express how wonderful it has been to work with you. Thank you for your patience as I stumbled through art direction and contracts and a special thanks for providing such gorgeous art for the cover and interior of *Death and the Taxman.*

I had some amazing first readers who provided crucial feedback, filled in plot holes, and were just all-around awesome to bounce ideas off of. Thank you Beth Hancock, Laughing Briar, Shannon Fox, Angelique Fawns, and Brittany Rainsdon. You made this story shine!

Thank you to my copy editor Dan Hilton for your sharp eye and red pen which made the manuscript look so beautifully professional.

I ran a Kickstarter in September 2023 to fund publication of this novel. The rousing success of that campaign would not have been possible without critical input, resources, and training from authors Wulf Moon (*How to Write a Howling Good Story*), Mark Leslie Lefebrve (*Wide for the Win*), Dean Wesley Smith (with his FREE online class *Kickstarter Best Practices for Fiction Writers*), and Anthea Sharp (*Kickstarter for Authors* and moderator of the Facebook group of the same name). Again, thank you for paying it forward.

Special thanks to editors Alex Shvatsman (*Unidentified Funny Objects 9*), Mike Jack Stoumbos (*Murderbirds*), and Danny Hankner (*Story Unlikely*) for donating books, stories, and subscriptions as Kickstarter backer rewards.

Last, but certainly not least, thank you to all the Kickstarter backers who helped bring *Death and the Taxman* to life! Funded at 595%! Your enthusiasm and generosity overwhelmed me. Thank you.

Kickstarter Backers: Adam Goldstein - Akis Linardos - Alex Fox - Alexander Barrett - Alexander Nirenberg - Alexandra Engrand - Alysha Cheah - Amy R. Guthington - Andrejs Zolotuhins - Andrew Dibble - Andrew Rector - Andrew Zerante - Angelique Fawns - Angy Garcilazo - Annmarie SanSevero - Antony Jordan - Ashley A - Ashley Funkhouser - Ashley Hamm - B. K. Wellman - BDan Fairchild - Ben - Ben Saylor - Ben Zerante - Bob Finegold - bookmarkedone - Brenda Hankins - Brendan Pease - Brian Mettlen - Brittany Hollander - Candice Lisle - Catherine Weaver - Cherise Papa - Cheyanne Barron - Chris Binns - Chris L.A. - Christina Minton - Cindy Temple - Conan64ds - Crystal Crawford - Cyra Uy - Daniel M. Cojocaru - Danny Hankner - Darren Lipman - Dave Holets - David K. Henrickson - Devin Miller - Dodie Sullivan - Dora Owens - Duke Holley - Dybbuk Klezmer - Dylan Pucilowski - Elizabeth Amico - Emmy and John LaTorre - Eric P. Kurniawan - Eric Stallsworth - Eron Wyngarde - Eva Jayet Alaminos - Evan Anderson - Franziska - Fred Wehling - Gaston Lamaitre - GmarkC - Gregory Tausch - Hadas Nahshon - Hamilton Hale - Heyley Ingram - J Delgado - J.R. Johnson - Jace Chretin - Jackie Payson - Jacky - Jacob Pérez - Jade Wildy - Jakub Narębski - James Davies - James McKlemurry - James Moon - James S. Caraballo - Jamie Lopez - Jamie Sonderman - Janessa Keeling - Jared S Campbell - Jarrod Williams - Jason Martinko - Jason Palmatier - Jeanna - Jenna Levitski - Jennifer Bair - Jennifer Eaton - Jennifer Lesh Fleck - Jenny Perry Carr - Jessica Enfante - John Eric Schleicher - Joshua Palmatier - K. Z.

Richards - Karen M - Karen Olmos - Kathryn McLeer - Kelly McMahon - Kelly Snyder - Kelsey Stenberg - Kendra Tornheim - Kenyon Wensing - Kevin A Davis - Laura Dion - Leana - Lee Wilson - Leigh Kimmel - Leon Glaser - Lily Raven - Lucille - Lucinda Duvall - Lucy - Luke Leveque - Manny Dresden - Marie Le Roux - Mark Leslie Lefebvre - Mark Lybrand - Mark Wyckstrom - Martin Greening - Martin L. Shoemaker - Matthew Pemble - Meredith Carstens - Micha Rieser - Michael the Horologist - Mighty V - MJ Henkels - Mordechai Boruch Gofman - Murph Mungovan - Natalie S - Nightwing Whitehead - Noele Clayton - P Byhmer - Pete Lead - Piet Wenings - R. M. Everhart - Rachael D Teuschler - Rachel Unger - Rachiel R. - Randy Heath - Rebecca E Treasure - Rikard Mennenga - Rob Steinberger - Robert Claney - Robert Lowe - Ruth Ann Orlansky - RW Miller - S. M. Kellat - Sam Hudson - Sam Parr - Sam Rutherford - Sandra Skalski - Scot Noel - Scott Casey - Scott M. Sands - Scott Tackett - Señor Neo - Shanda - Shannon Fox - Shanon M. Brown - Shean Pao - Spencer Sekulin - Stephannie Tallent - Stephen Dierks - Stephen Kotowych - Stephen W. Buchanan - Steve & Beckey Sanchez - Steve and Carolyn Stein - Steve Pantazis - Steven Clark - Tech Support lvl 1&2 (Petersons) -

Terry Ebaugh - Thomas Legg - Tim Hankins - TJ Knight - Tom Hodder - Tony McCowan - Tracy Hughes - Tyler Tarter - WaterNai - Wingnut - Wulf Moon Enterprises - Yelena Crane - Zach Carter

To everyone I forgot to mention, to the writing community that has provided such stalwart support, to the friends and family who have cheered me on, and to the short story markets who keep publishing my quirky upbeat stories:

THANK YOU!

David

ABOUT THE AUTHOR

Award-winning author David Hankins writes from the thriving cornfields of Iowa where he lives with his wife, daughter, and two dragons disguised as cats. His writing began in the oral tradition of convincing his daughter to Go To Sleep with inventive stories. That usually backfired. After years of Just One More Story, David began transcribing his midnight ramblings in an attempt to keep his storylines straight. Children are ruthless about mistakes in their fairy tales. David writes lighthearted speculative fiction because that's what he loves to read and—this is the important bit—there's not nearly enough humor in the world. He aims to change that, one story at a time. You can find him at https://davidhankins.com